WHEN SCANDAL CAME TO TOWN

Scandalous Sons - Book 3

ADELE CLEE

This is a work of fiction. All names, characters, places and incidents are products of the author's imagination. All characters are fictitious and any resemblance to real persons, living or dead, is purely coincidental.

When Scandal Came to Town

ISBN-13: 978-1-9162774-0-3

CHAPTER ONE

THE SERPENTINE, HYDE PARK

Cold air raced over Cassandra Mills' bare skin. It was not like the refreshing breeze one experienced in the height of summer. It did not settle her heart or drag a soft sigh from her lips. It did not soothe her spirit. Heavens no. The icy gust swept over her like frozen fingers determined to startle and shock. It sent her pulse soaring, sent her heart into a sudden state of panic. Had she been at home in the comfort of her poster bed, she would have snatched the blankets and snuggled down inside the protective cocoon. Warm. Safe. But she was not at home. And from the aches and pains plaguing her body, the hard surface was definitely not her plush bed.

She tried to open her eyes, but it was as if she had lids of lead. She inhaled, hoping for a clue to her surroundings, and caught the smell of damp earth and the hint of sulphur that always accompanied the early morning fog.

Morning?

No!

She recalled nothing since last night. Nothing since the music, the dancing, the fruit punch that shouldn't have made her dizzy. Yes. The sweet aftertaste of orgeat lemonade still coated her lips. And something else, something sickly, something dangerously potent.

Mustering an ounce of strength, she stretched her feeble limbs. Nausea roiled in her stomach. The pounding in her head would not abate. The cold set her teeth chattering. She reached out looking for support, a means to help her clamber to her feet, but her fingers slipped through naught but dew-soaked grass.

A park. She must be in a park.

But which one?

The distant trickle of water caught her attention.

Hyde Park?

Somehow she lifted her heavy lids, though by all that was holy she wished she hadn't. Reality hit hard. So hard all the air escaped her lungs, leaving her panting and breathless. Lord help her! The lucid dream had proved kinder than this terrifying nightmare.

Hyde Park!

She almost laughed at the pun.

Lying barely clothed and helpless amid the acres of parkland, she had no hope of remaining undiscovered. There was nowhere to go, nowhere to hide. Even the morning fog lacked spirit and clung to the ground in ghostly wisps. To her right, tall trees loomed like disapproving matrons ready to hurl a torrent of insults, ready to banish her from every social event of the season. The Serpentine curled around to the left. A snake in the grass. The devil's spawn there to taunt the foolish woman who had somehow eaten the forbidden fruit.

And yet she couldn't remember.

Why couldn't she remember?

If she could scramble to her feet, she might find her way out of the park before the first riders took to the Row. But how would she navigate the mile back to Cavendish Square wearing nothing but her chemise?

As if matters couldn't get any worse, the rumble of thunder

overhead drew her gaze skyward. Was the Lord waiting to strike down the wicked harlot? Was he about to send a deluge of rain to wash away her sins?

But she soon discovered that the resounding noise was not a warning foretelling of horrid weather, but the pounding of horse's hooves galloping across the parkland.

Her heart stopped beating for a second or two.

Oh, so many times she'd felt the crippling impotence of her sex. As a woman, she'd stood powerless while her father told her who to befriend, what functions to attend, who to marry. None-theless, nothing compared to this sense of utter uselessness—this desperate despair.

Had she managed to rouse a sliver of optimism she might have hoped the rider was a godly man. Someone who saw that she was the victim of a heinous crime. Someone who saw good-ness when he looked deeply into her eyes. But as the rider came charging towards her on his impressive black stallion, she knew the devil had sent his disciple.

Benedict Cavanagh—the bane of her existence—brought his horse to a crashing halt and dismounted with the same athletic grace he did most things.

Shame brought fire to her cheeks. But then he always had such a marked effect on her senses. Why did he have to look so sinfully handsome in his midnight-blue coat? How did he manage to heat her insides with nothing more than a concerned stare?

"Cassandra?" He crouched beside her, his muscular thighs straining against his breeches. "What the devil's happened to you?" While shock marred his velvet voice, she heard a faint hint of kindness, a kindness he'd shown her long ago, before hate replaced the love in their hearts.

Embarrassment kept her lips pursed.

He removed his top hat and thrust a hand through his golden hair as his expression turned grave.

That's when she knew.
She was dead or ruined.
Either way, it amounted to the same.

CHAPTER TWO

Many times during their verbal spats, Benedict had prayed Cassandra Mills would receive her comeuppance. She made a point of belittling him in front of his friends. Her unkind remarks hit like the sharp stab of a blade. And though he offered the same cutting retorts, she always drew first blood.

On rare occasions, he caught a fleeting glimpse of the Cassandra he once knew. The affectionate girl with a vitality that stole his breath. The girl who had kissed him under the willow tree, who had given him an acorn as a gift and told him that majestic things grow from the smallest beginnings.

Now, as she lay on the grass in nothing but a dirty chemise, her bedraggled golden curls tumbling from her coiffure, he felt neither love nor hatred. Shock rendered him insensible. Numb.

But then she opened her mouth, and the usual vile diatribe followed. "You! I should have known you would plan something like this." Her lips thinned into an ugly sneer. She tried to push up to a sitting position but lacked the strength in her limbs.

The fact she thought so little of him stung like the lash of a whip.

"Let me help you." He wasn't a monster. He wouldn't wish

this on any woman. But when he reached out to offer assistance, she found the wherewithal to slap his hand away.

"Don't touch me!"

Once, they'd stolen every opportunity to make physical contact, a secret embrace, the light brush of their fingers when no one was looking.

"What did you do?" She rubbed her sunken eyes, drew a hand down her deathly pale cheek. "Did you f-follow me to Lord Craven's ball?" Speaking seemed to drain her energy, and she had to stop to catch her breath. "Did you kidnap me and ply me with laudanum, intent on ruining me to get your revenge?"

Anger pushed to the fore, mingling with an old pain that had never healed. Their relationship amounted to nothing more than a bitter war. If only one of them could find the courage to play peacekeeper.

"You think I did this to you?" Disdain coated his words. "You think revenge matters so much to me that I would ruin an innocent, delve to the worst depths of depravity?"

"You're the prince of depravity. Everyone says so." She managed to sit up without his assistance. "The demimonde is your kingdom. What else should a lady expect from a man who beds whores?"

With a need to defend his position, he almost said that he'd rather bed a whore than bed her, but that was untrue. He might have said that she'd driven him to seek pleasure in a place where people abandoned their emotions at the front door. But then she would need to defend his attack, and they would be forever going around in circles, lashing out, parrying against the next killer blow.

"Perhaps depravity is in my blood." His father was most definitely no angel. "I was born out of wedlock. A fact you bring to my attention at every given opportunity." He would never be good enough for a blue blood. "Regardless of how you ended up here, people will cast similar aspersions on you."

A sob caught in her throat, but she fought it back with her

usual expression of steely reserve. "This is what you wanted, what you've longed for all these years. Ruining my reputation is the only way you can hurt me."

A weary sigh left his lips. "Cassandra, I had nothing to do with what happened to you. If I did, would I not be gloating? The triumphant look on my face would be hard to disguise. And why would I risk your father's wrath, or my father's for that matter?"

That said, the Earl of Tregarth would forgive his illegitimate son anything. Cassandra's father, the Earl of Worthen, would string Benedict up at the Seven Dials and spill his innards.

Cassandra glared at him. "Then what brought you to Hyde Park at dawn? Surely you don't expect me to believe it's a coincidence."

"I don't give a damn what you believe." He delved into the inside pocket of his coat and withdrew the letter. "This arrived anonymously last night. As you can see, curiosity brought me here this morning."

The sender knew how to pique a man's interest. A surprise to surpass all others awaited him in Hyde Park. A sight not to be missed. The vermillion seal bore no identifying marks. The handwriting appeared nondescript.

With trembling fingers she snatched the letter, and he noted the scratches on her hands. She must have fought the person who had practically stripped her naked. As she peeled back the folds and scanned the missive, her whole body shook. A tear trickled down her cheek. How odd that a single drop of water could wring knots in his stomach.

"But I don't understand." With a look of confusion and utter defeat, she reread the neatly penned words. "Who would send you a letter telling you to come here at dawn? It can only be the person who did this to me. Someone who cares so much for you they would give you my ruination as a gift."

The thought had not occurred to him. An image of Mrs Crandall flashed into his mind. The fiery-haired matron of the demimonde made no secret of her lust for him. To say she was somewhat obsessed was an understatement. Had she done this to prove her devotion? To tempt him into bed? Surely not.

"This doesn't have to be your ruination."

Cassandra jerked her head and snorted. "Blessed saints, tell me you're not about to propose marriage."

"Marriage? Do I look like an imbecile?" He wouldn't make the same mistake twice.

"Then what are you proposing?"

Benedict glanced back over his shoulder. There wasn't a soul in the park. "Let me take you home. You can bury your head in my coat. We'll enter your father's house via the mews. You can sneak in through the servants' entrance. Surely your maid will rally to your aid."

She blinked so many times he couldn't help but admire the way her long lashes fluttered against her pale skin. "Despite everything that's occurred between us, you're willing to help me?"

The devil on his shoulder shouted for him to climb back on his horse and leave her there. Let her face the fact other people despised her, too. Let her spend her life living with the scandal. Was that not a fitting punishment for the way she had treated him?

But he was a scoundrel with a conscience.

A rogue with a heart.

"Perhaps the person who sent me here expected me to celebrate your downfall." It wouldn't have been Wycliff or Trent. His friends knew how much he despised Cassandra Mills, but they were men with hearts, too, men he'd trust with his life. "Whoever sent the letter doesn't know me at all."

It had to be Mrs Crandall.

"And if Lord Murray loves you as he ought," Benedict continued, "he will marry you regardless of any whispers of a scandal." When he first heard of their betrothal it had cleaved his insides in two. He'd used women and brandy to numb his senses.

The method had served him well so far. "The sooner he marries you the better."

"Timothy is a good man," she agreed. "He would never go back on his word."

Not like her.

He wondered if she could see the warring emotions playing on his face. But then she looked at life through superficial eyes now.

"One must hope that no one saw you in this dishevelled state last night. You should press your father to bring Murray up to the mark. Today."

Gratitude swam in her eyes. It made him feel more uncomfortable than when witnessing her disdain. She wrapped her arms across her chest and shivered. He had been so focused on not staring at the pert nipples pressing against the fine chemise, it had not occurred to him that she must be cold.

Benedict stood. He shrugged out of his coat and draped it around her shoulders, half expecting her to toss the garment away like a filthy rag. She didn't. She thrust her arms into the sleeves, drew the edges across her chest and gave a satisfied sigh.

"Come." He needed to put some distance between them before the old memories returned to plague his waking hours, to haunt his dreams. "Let me help you up onto my horse. We should leave here before the first morning riders venture out onto the Row."

"Yes, you're right."

"You agree? There's a novelty."

She slipped her cold, dainty hand into his, and a lightning bolt of awareness shot straight to his heart. Cursed saints. Was Satan out to torture him for being weak, for not leaving her to suffer her fate?

"The muscles in my legs lack strength," she said, though her gaze lingered on their clasped hands. "I'm not sure I can stand."

"Then I will help you." He suppressed a groan of frustration.

The last thing he wanted was to touch her, not when he would feel the lush curves he remembered.

"Why are you being so kind?" She gripped his outstretched arm. "One might think you've arranged this so you can play the errant knight. Are you so desperate to prove your worth?"

"For the love of God, Cassandra, I had nothing to do with this debacle." Anger flared. Even in her hour of need she had to taunt him with his illegitimacy. She always spoke as if it was his fault Tregarth had taken a mistress. Was it his fault his mother died in childbirth before she might marry, too? "But one more cruel word and I swear I shall leave you here to perish."

The flash of fear in her blue eyes was the closest he would get to an apology.

"Wrap your arms around my neck, and I shall haul you to your feet." The sooner he dealt with the problem, the sooner he could return to the comfort of his bed. "Fatigue makes a person feeble. I suspect you've spent hours lying in the cold. Your maid will draw you a hot bath and prepare a herbal decoction. Both will act as a restorative."

"I suppose a rake who spends most nights carousing until dawn knows how to stave off a cold."

The snide remark forced him to snatch his arm back. His head roared for him to leave. His heart clambered to her defence. For his sanity he could not tolerate her company a second longer.

Benedict swung around, but Cassandra grabbed his coattails and cried, "Forgive me. Please, Benedict, don't leave without me. Foolish words fall from my mouth before my mind engages. Don't abandon me. Not now."

The irony of the situation almost made him laugh.

Had she forgotten how easily she'd cast him aside?

"Please, Benedict." His given name fell softly from her lips. "Take me home. Timothy will marry me, and you need never see me again."

Benedict closed his eyes for a few seconds and inhaled. In

some perverse way, he would rather tolerate her abuse than suffer an estrangement.

Bloody fool!

Ride away and don't look back.

"If you ever cared for me at all, please help me now."

Ever cared for her? She may as well have gripped a blade and driven the cold steel through his heart. A rage like nothing he'd felt before crashed through him in violent waves. Painful words formed. Vicious words. They danced like the devil on his tongue, but he would never give her the satisfaction of knowing how much he'd suffered. He might be an illegitimate bastard, but today he would be the considerate gentleman.

Without another word, he turned on his heel, gritted his teeth and scooped her up into his arms.

She clung to him like a fragile child. Helpless. Insecure. Small fingers clutched at his shirt sleeves as if she feared she might fall.

When she opened her mouth to speak, he said, "No more. Not today."

She nodded, and though they stood surrounded by the vast expanse of the park, the air proved suffocating.

Twice she tried to place her foot in the stirrup, but she lacked the strength to pull herself up.

Benedict stood rooted to the spot—contemplating what the hell to do—when the thunder of horses' hooves pounding the ground captured his attention. Two men rode towards them. Two more cantered closely behind.

Panic brought a sharp pain to his throat when the riders came into view and he recognised them as Lord Forrester, Laird McCreath, Lord Purcell and Lord Drummond. Powerful men. Influential men. Drummond had ambitions in government with aims to be the next Lord Chancellor. Forrester's wife was the most notorious gossip in the *ton*. The Scottish laird was a friend of Benedict's father, and Purcell sought every opportunity to belittle his peers.

Like the Four Horsemen of the Apocalypse set to bring certain destruction, they stopped but a few feet away. The shocked whispers and sly smirks confirmed they'd drawn the obvious conclusions. They'd named Benedict the rakish seducer, Cassandra the naive chit who had fallen for his charms.

"Could you not find somewhere warmer to conduct your liaison, Cavanagh?" Forrester, a man of sixty with ridiculous grey whiskers, chuckled.

Cassandra shivered. She clung to him and buried her face in the crook of his neck.

"No doubt it's too late to hide your identity," he whispered into her hair. "But don't show them your face." He raised his chin and scanned the four men. "What brings you to Hyde Park at this ungodly hour?" Deep down, he knew the reason for their dawn outing. Why else would four gentlemen veer from the Row and ride closer to the Serpentine?

"Would you believe we all received the same letter?" Drummond, a man of forty with cherub cheeks and an ever-growing paunch, drew the missive from his coat pocket and flapped it in the air. "It seems we were all invited to witness the scandal of the season."

Had Benedict not been in such a dire predicament, he'd have told them all to go to hell. Ridiculed them for being gossiping fishwives. But he could do nothing other than listen to their mocking taunts.

Whoever orchestrated the event had picked the players wisely. Mrs Crandall knew many men's secrets. Mrs Crandall had the power to blackmail those hypocritical lords in society and force them to perform wicked acts.

"You're a brave man," Purcell added with a smile of contempt. "Worthen will see you on the next ship to the Americas once he learns you've ruined his daughter."

Damnation!

How the devil did they know?

"You're mistaken," Benedict replied with an air of arrogance. "Worthen's daughter is the last woman I would bed."

Cassandra stiffened in his arms. From the erratic jerks of her body, he knew she was crying.

"Och, there's no point hiding the fact. The letter reveals the lady's name." McCreath drew his hand down his wiry red beard and sighed. "You'll need Tregarth's help if you're to survive this scandal, laddie."

Benedict saw no point in minding his manners now. No point in attempting to disguise Cassandra's identity. "Then I'm sure you've all seen enough to send you scurrying back into the cesspit eager to spread your deadly tales."

Purcell's frog eyes bulged. "Says the gutter rat to his superiors. Tregarth is a fool. He should have cast this ill-bred reprobate aside long ago."

McCreath threw Purcell a hard stare. "Mind your tongue. Highland lairds make a trophy from the ballocks of a man who insults his friends."

It took a few seconds for Purcell to decide how to respond. He took one look at McCreath's broad shoulders, shook his head and said, "It's one thing to whore your way around town, Cavanagh. Another to ruin an innocent and still expect people to open their doors to you."

"As always, Lord Purcell, you judge a man guilty without giving him a fair trial." Benedict lowered Cassandra down slowly until her bare feet touched the grass. He slid a strong arm around her back to keep her upright and held her close to his chest. "Men like you have no interest in the truth. Men like you prey on other people's weaknesses to divert attention away from your own."

"Perhaps you should stand as a spokesman for the Whigs, Mr Cavanagh," Drummond said with a chuckle. "We need men willing to speak for the downtrodden."

Purcell had clearly heard enough. With a muttered curse, he edged his horse around, whipped the reins and galloped back to the Row. Forrester had the means to supply his wife with the latest gossip and so was hot on Lord Purcell's heels.

"Have heart, Mr Cavanagh," Drummond said. "If you're a clever man, you might turn this scandal to your advantage." And with that, he rode away, too.

McCreath nudged his mount closer. "Do you need help lifting the lass onto your horse?"

Cassandra shook her head. She slid her arms around Benedict's waist and pressed her face to his neckcloth. The feel of her gripping him tightly sent his world spinning.

"No, though I thank you for challenging Purcell."

"I'll have no man speak ill of your father. Aye, certainly not a weasel like Purcell." McCreath glanced at the lady locked in Benedict's embrace. "What will you do now?"

He would do the only thing he could under the circumstances. He would return to Cavendish Square and explain the situation to Lord Worthen. Benedict was no longer the fearful boy ashamed of his lineage. "At present, I must focus on leaving the park posthaste. After that … well … I imagine once the gossip wheel starts turning, events will take the expected course."

McCreath inclined his head at Benedict's vague reply. "I can return with a carriage, should the lass prefer to head north of the border. An elopement would be the simple solution."

Benedict snorted. Nothing in his life was simple.

Cassandra gripped the back of Benedict's waistcoat in response. The lady had no desire to marry him at all, let alone travel three hundred miles for the pleasure.

"Again, I thank you for the offer, McCreath, but I must see the lady safely home." Curious as to the contents of McCreath's letter, he said, "Strange that I, too, received a letter prompting me to ride here this morning. Mine specifically said to arrive at the Serpentine at dawn. How convenient you arrived twenty minutes later."

Could it be a coincidence?

"The instructions said to meet at the Cumberland Gate just after the break of dawn."

The Cumberland Gate? And he'd been told to come to Hyde Park Corner via Piccadilly.

"Aye, we might have arrived ten minutes sooner," McCreath continued, "but Forrester tried to persuade us to leave and then argued with Purcell."

Cassandra Mills' ruination was a carefully constructed plan that might never have come to fruition had they all ignored the letters. But then the sender had been extremely persuasive. Indeed, to achieve the desired result, the villain needed but one man out of the four to nibble the bait.

Cassandra tugged on his waistcoat and whispered, "Take me home, Benedict."

"We should leave, McCreath, before someone else stumbles upon this carefully constructed scene." Lord knows what other devilish plans the mysterious kidnapper had up his sleeve.

McCreath steered his horse to face the parkland. "I'll not keep this matter from your father. Not when Purcell will take pleasure informing him that I bore witness to the scandal."

"Do what you must." Tregarth would hear of it from other sources soon enough.

McCreath inclined his head before flicking the reins and urging his horse into a canter.

Benedict wasted no time in assisting Cassandra up onto his black stallion. She seemed a little sturdier on her feet. The strength had returned to her muscles, though her red-rimmed eyes and puffy face spoke of emotions wrought with panic and fear. He settled behind her, and she snuggled into his coat and rested her head against his chest.

Lord have mercy!

"I don't think the day could get any worse," she said, her voice as broken as her spirit.

He didn't want to lie. Nor could he say this was only the beginning of her nightmare. "You're a strong woman, Cassandra." Strong enough to cast him aside after all her promises. "You will find a way through this mess and rise victorious."

Her spine stiffened, and she grew rigid against him. At first, he thought her reaction stemmed from the distress of leaving the park and venturing out onto the street. But after muttering something wholly unladylike, she said, "When I discover who did this, I will make his life a living hell."

After all she had put him through, he could believe that.

CHAPTER THREE

The deathly silence slipped around Cassandra's throat like the reaper's bony fingers, ready to squeeze the last breath from her lungs. While being half-naked in Hyde Park proved terrifying, nothing chilled her blood like her father's merciless stare.

Benedict Cavanagh sat confidently in the chair beside her, his back straight, chin raised. "Would you care to see the letter I received from the wicked conspirator?" The steely edge to his voice cut through the oppressive air. A fool could see that he loathed the earl, almost as much as he loathed her.

The Earl of Worthen studied Benedict through cold flint-grey eyes, eyes that made one shiver even in the height of summer. With his small mouth lost in a sour expression, her father flicked his fingers impatiently and motioned for the letter.

Benedict did not retaliate or sneer at the rude gesture. A wry smile played on his lips as he reached into his coat pocket and withdrew the folded note. He placed it on the desk slightly out of the earl's reach.

Cassandra's thoughts should have turned to the evil words written to secure her ruination. Yet she became lost in the memory of how comforting it felt being wrapped in Benedict's warm coat. His unique scent—the divine smell that had faded from the secret letters hidden in her drawer—still filled her head when she inhaled.

"How the devil do I know you didn't bribe someone to write this damning note? That this isn't a vile scheme to trap my daughter into marriage?" The earl's irate voice jolted Cassandra from her reverie. Anger turned her father's cheeks beetroot-red. "Men like you hunt for ways to advance the social ladder."

"Men like me?" Benedict mocked. "You mean illegitimate sons of peers who should be left to scavenge in the gutter?"

"I mean men who have no place in polite society."

"You tolerated my company once."

Benedict spoke of a time when their fathers were friends, of a summer spent in Brighton, a Christmas spent at the Earl of Tregarth's estate near Bath. Happier times. Wonderful times.

"Yes, in private, and until you made me aware of your foolish designs to marry Cassandra."

"Then you did me a great service," Benedict countered. "On reflection, I thank the Lord I am illegitimate, else you might have taken me into your fold and sought to control me as you do your daughter."

"Why, you spurious son of a wanton!" The earl thumped the desk with his fist. "If you were the last man on earth, I wouldn't let Cassandra marry you."

"Good. As I have no intention of marrying her either." Benedict brushed a hand through his mop of golden hair. "I have dealt with self-righteous prigs my whole life. Throw your tantrums. Hurl your abuse. Nothing you can say can hurt me. I bow to no one. Perhaps that's what frustrates you."

Cassandra simply stared at the man beside her. His strength of character filled her with awe. Despite everything her father had said, Benedict Cavanagh possessed a duke's bearing. She threw a suspicious glance at the earl, the man who had convinced her that Lord Tregarth's son was a rogue controlled by his ungodly appetites, a man lacking influence and power.

Of course, she should have known what would happen next. Men obsessed with their own superiority took their tempers out on those they deemed weakest.

The earl turned his anger on her. "Do you see what you've created? Have I taught you nothing these last twenty-three years? Behave like a harlot and the world will treat you like one. Tell me, did you leave the ball to meet with Cavanagh last night? Did you concoct this story after giving yourself to him like a back-alley whore?"

Cassandra sat dumbstruck. Her mind was a muddled mess. She remembered visiting the ladies' retiring room and nothing else thereafter. As she tried to rouse a response to the dreadful accusations, Benedict interjected on her behalf.

"Must you speak to her in that vile way?"

"Don't tell me how to speak to my own daughter."

"While a wealth of animosity exists between us—and she is the last person I would expect to defend—do you not think she has suffered enough? Where is your compassion? Where are the words of comfort?" Benedict glanced at her for the first time since he'd settled his hands on her waist and helped her down from his horse. "If this is how gentlemen behave, I thank God I'm illegitimate."

The earl jumped to his feet. "Get out!" Saliva bubbled at the corners of his mouth. "Leave this house and never return. Murray is a gentleman and will marry her regardless of this fiasco, and I have the power to silence men like Purcell."

Benedict did not argue. Wearing a mischievous smile, he rose with languid grace. "Perhaps you should invest your time trying to establish who wants to hurt your daughter." He snatched the letter off the desk and thrust it into his coat pocket. "Perhaps you have enemies who will stop at nothing to cause your family pain."

Though Cassandra had remained silent for the last ten minutes, the need to say something forced her to stand. "I am assured you are an unsuspecting player in this spiteful game, Mr

Cavanagh. Consequently, I cannot let you leave without thanking you for your assistance this morning." It was the nicest thing she had said to him in years. So why did the words cause a painful pang in her heart?

Benedict swallowed deeply though did not make eye contact. "You must send word to Lord Murray at once. He's your only hope of salvaging something of your reputation."

The lie fell easily from his lips. She was beyond redemption, would forever bear the mark of this betrayal. Only love could save her now. And Lord Murray had professed love more times than she could count.

"Perhaps Tregarth orchestrated this whole affair, desperate to give you the only thing you truly desire," her father snapped. "Well, you won't have it. Do you hear? Murray will step up to the mark. You can be certain of that."

For the first time since Benedict had entered the study, Cassandra saw a flicker of doubt in his bold blue eyes. The Earl of Tregarth wouldn't stoop so low. Would he?

"I sincerely hope Murray is a gentleman. The sort who understands the value of love." Benedict did not incline his head as he took his leave, did not take her hand or offer a bow. Why would he when he despised them to their core?

As she listened to the clip of Benedict's booted steps recede along the hall, she felt more alone, more exposed than she had in Hyde Park. The stomach-churning silence left her dreading her father's next comment.

"You will wait in your bedchamber until Lord Murray arrives." The earl rounded the desk, his teeth bared. "You're not to leave this house without my permission. Is that clear?"

A mocking snort escaped her. "Have no fear. I doubt I shall ever leave the house again." The thought of walking the streets —every head whipping in her direction, every wicked whisper carrying her name—made her nauseous.

"I'll send for a physician to confirm you're still intact.

Should he find otherwise, then you may as well return to Hyde Park to peddle your wares."

A physician?

Hate reared like a spitting serpent in her chest. No matter what she did, she could never make this man proud. Would he ever forgive the fact her mother died giving her life? Would he ever accept that every attempt to sire an heir brought death and devastation? It was the one thing he had in common with the Earl of Tregarth. The glaring difference was that Tregarth loved his son.

Knowing it was futile to argue, she bowed her head and made for the door.

"I shall ask you one question, and you will tell me the truth!" Her father's booming voice stopped her dead in her tracks. "I will know if you're lying. Turn to face me, girl. Let me see if wickedness dances in your eyes."

Cassandra swung around and lifted her chin. She would have married anyone to escape this house. But her father demanded she choose Lord Murray for her husband, despite the gentleman insisting on a lengthy betrothal.

"Ask your question," she said, knowing it would be like another barbed arrow to her damaged heart.

"Did you send the letter to Cavanagh? Did you send the letters to all of them in the hope the bastard would marry you?"

"You think I planned my own ruination?" Good God. She expected the worst from him but did not expect that. "You think I stripped off my clothes and lay cold and helpless on the grass? You think I am that devious, that callous I would trap a man into marriage?"

The earl looked her keenly in the eyes, the lines on his forehead deepening. "You loved the filthy guttersnipe once."

"Don't call him that. I would have perished in the park were it not for him." A storm of feelings swirled in her chest. "But yes, I loved him once. Not anymore, due to your wicked intervention." Her shoulders sagged and water welled in her eyes.

"You taught me to believe that reputation is everything. Why would I damage the only thing I had left?"

Keen to prevent him from seeing her so distraught, she hurried from the room, ran to her bedchamber and slammed the door. Only then did she crumple into a heap and sob until there were no more tears left to shed.

Three hours passed before Dr Hadley arrived to perform his degrading examination, to meddle and probe and declare her untouched. Five hours later, the earl summoned her to the study to face Lord Murray, the only man with the power to ease her pain and make minor repairs to her tattered reputation.

The earl's loud voice reached her ears long before she reached the stairs. The maid and the footman listening at the study door scattered upon hearing Cassandra's descent. Although snooping was an accepted pastime for society ladies, she would rather look Lord Murray in the eyes when he delivered his verdict. Still, a terrible sense of foreboding prevented her from turning the doorknob.

After a moment spent convincing herself there were good men in the world, she patted her hair and entered the room. Both men came to their feet. Both men wore a look of anxious frustration.

A lock of dark hair fell over Timothy's brow as he inclined his head. "Cassandra, forgive me. I would have come sooner, but Lord Mendleson kept me at the club. He is not the sort of man one leaves halfway through a conversation."

"No, of course not," she said, her smile as weak as Timothy's chin. Would Benedict Cavanagh have sat drinking port and discussing politics while his betrothed suffered the worst kind of humiliation? "But you're here now, and I cannot tell you how glad I am to see you."

Timothy's thin lips twitched as he struggled to meet her gaze.

"Your father said you've been the victim of a cruel plot to undermine his position."

"The version Murray heard at the club told a different story," her father snapped. "Some men have nothing better to do than manipulate events to suit their purpose. Thankfully, we're intelligent enough to see through their wicked games."

"Lord Purcell said he found you half-naked in the arms of Tregarth's son."

The comment almost made her retch. More so because she knew that was reason enough for Timothy to withdraw his marriage proposal.

"Tregarth's son happened to stumble upon me in a distressed state mere moments before Lord Purcell arrived. As my father said, someone sought to stage the event with the express purpose of harming my family."

"I see." Timothy did not look convinced. "Still, you can see why it poses a problem."

He stood, staring at nothing. It was the first time she had ever noticed his insipid eyes, eyes that lacked any real expression. Even when he'd professed his love, the spoken words conveyed meaning, not his countenance. Indeed, his whole bearing lacked the unwavering strength one observed in Benedict Cavanagh.

"The physician has certified the girl is intact. Does that not prove that some devil fabricated this whole event?" Never had her father looked so nervous. "I can arrange for a special licence, but perhaps the best course of action is to take Cassandra north. A wedding in Scotland will suffice, and a few weeks spent out of town will steal the wind from the gossips' sails."

Good Lord! She hadn't thought it possible to feel more helpless, more demeaned than she had this morning. Hearing her father practically beg Lord Murray to marry her left her thoroughly ashamed.

"There's no reason to rush into anything." Timothy shook his head. "No reason to panic."

"No reason!" her father bellowed. "God damn it, man, the chit's life is in tatters and you want to delay?"

Of course he wanted to delay. A gentleman did not marry a lady embroiled in a scandal. Lady Murray's daughter-in-law must be as pure as the driven snow. Morally unsullied. A paragon of virtue.

"The situation requires some reflection." Timothy shuffled uncomfortably. "I have ambitions in government. A man in my position must be mindful who he marries."

Now Cassandra knew why the lord wore his collars so high and his cravat tied in so complicated a knot it might well strangle him if he jerked suddenly. A spineless man needed help to keep his head upright.

"And what of love?" she dared ask, eager to hear yet another bumbling excuse.

Timothy frowned. "You know as well as I do, love plays no part in society marriages. History books rarely mention the wives of successful men."

"So you do love me?"

"Love you? I adore you, but countries are not built on love, Cassandra."

If Benedict Cavanagh loved a woman, would he see her thrown to the wolves to satisfy his ambition? When Benedict professed his love all those years ago, she had seen the glaring truth in his eyes. Timothy's eyes were a dim blue when he spoke about anything other than politics.

"Surely you can see how difficult this is for me," the lord pleaded. Anyone would think he'd been found drugged and semi-naked in Hyde Park. "Every decision I make must be done with extreme thought and care." He turned his attention to her father. "A man cannot defy the standards set by society's upper echelons."

"She's the daughter of an earl, not a blasted market hawker. By rights, she could have set her sights higher than a mere baron. But your ambitions are the reason I wanted to forge an alliance."

Insulting her betrothed was hardly conducive to achieving one's goal. Besides, she would rather suffer eternal shame than take this disloyal fool for a husband.

"It is of no consequence." Somehow she found the strength to speak without her voice breaking. "Suffice to say I free you from your obligation, Lord Murray."

"What? Be quiet, Cassandra." The earl stared down his patrician nose. "You're the reason we're in this godforsaken predicament. If you cannot speak sense, don't speak at all."

The tightening of her throat preceded the onset of tears. She didn't want to cry in front of Timothy, but the first drops splashed onto her cheeks, and she had to dash them away. "May I remind you both, I am the victim of a crime. A crime perpetrated against me because of some wrong you have committed, Father." Anger surfaced, and she gritted her teeth at Timothy. "Or perhaps Lady Murray arranged my ruination because she has designs on another lady for your wife."

Timothy's cheeks puffed. "I know you're upset, Cassandra, but I'll not have a bad word spoken against my mother."

"Upset?" *Devastated* was the better word, although that didn't even begin to describe how she felt. "Upset is what one experiences when they have snagged their new dress."

"You're hardly in a position to criticise a man for making a wrong choice."

Cassandra stood dumbfounded.

Not because both men were cruel to belittle and shame her. Not because the life she knew was lost to her now. But because standing amid the ruins and the debris felt oddly liberating. What was there to fear when one occupied the lowest order? From here on in things could only improve. Indeed, in rebuilding a life from the ashes, she might make her own rules, choose her own destiny.

"Perhaps you're right, Lord Murray." She refused to use his

given name now. "There seems little point continuing this conversation as you have made me acutely aware of your position. You may hurry home to your mother and reassure her that you've slipped free from scandal's noose."

Despite the earl's furious objections and hostile outbursts, Lord Murray scampered away as fast as his legs could carry him.

"Have you taken leave of your senses?" The earl slapped his palms on the desk, leaned forward and glared. "Damn foolish chit. I could have brought Murray up to the mark."

"You know how these scandals play out. Reputation is often considered more important than a title." As a man obsessed with his own superiority, the earl expected people to forgive his daughter anything. "If the future of this country rests upon weak men like Lord Murray, God help us all."

Cassandra listened to her father berate the lord he'd hand-picked to be her husband, the lord he now regarded with disgust, repugnance and utter contempt.

The earl sneered. "I shall do everything in my power to see Murray pays a hefty price for rejecting you."

There was little point telling her father that his need for vengeance might be the reason she was in such dire straits. "And I shall do everything in my power to ensure I find the person responsible for kidnapping me last night." Though the thought proved daunting, it would give her a purpose, something on which to focus her mind.

"Chadderton is on the hunt for a bride. The old fool is in desperate need of an heir and will overlook your situation for the right price."

"No!" The word flew from her mouth before her mind engaged. "I'm of age to choose my own husband." She could flee to the country, live a quiet life of spinsterhood, but she had too much heart, too much spirit for that. "If he will have me, I want to marry Mr Cavanagh."

"Cavanagh?" The earl spat. "How many more times must I

tell you? The boy is a degenerate. His descent into a life of dissipation is well noted. And what possible benefit is that to me?"

"Tregarth would be a powerful ally. Mr Cavanagh will inherit a substantial fortune." Not that she cared about that. "Can you not overlook the unfortunate circumstances of his birth?"

"I can no more overlook it now than I could five years ago."

A determination to fight saw her ball her hands into fists. "Tregarth will do anything to secure his son's happiness. If I marry Mr Cavanagh, the earl will work tirelessly to see all whispers of a scandal squashed. It's more than an adequate solution to the problem."

"You'll not marry Tregarth's bastard!"

"Then I shall not marry at all."

CHAPTER FOUR

Hot water soothed the tension from Benedict's taut muscles, but it did nothing to ease the ache in his chest. He'd thought he was finished with Cassandra Mills, thought he had a grasp on the erratic emotions that accompanied the problems of the past. But having her cling to him, distraught and helpless, played havoc with his insides.

He relaxed back in his bath, surrounded by the soft glow of candlelight, and closed his eyes only for vivid memories to bombard his mind. Today was not the first time he had played errant knight. He had been the one to carry her spaniel home when the dog caught its foot in a poacher's trap. The one to carry her on his back when she twisted her ankle. The one who fixed the rope swing, who caught her every time she fell.

And yet despite that, he wasn't the one she wanted.

Benedict reached for the brass bell on the small trestle table beside him. One ring brought the footman into the large dressing room.

"Fill and light my meerschaum, Perkins, and hand it to me, would you?" Benedict gestured to the rosewood tobacco box on the chest of drawers. "And bring my best bottle of claret."

Perkins set about his duties, handing Benedict the pipe

before heading to the wine cellar. Upon his return, Benedict noted that Perkins carried two crystal goblets on the silver tray. He was about to question the footman when the Earl of Tregarth appeared in the doorway. His father strode into the room, dragged a chair up to the bathtub and dropped onto the padded seat.

"I hear you've had an eventful morning?" Tregarth wore a permanent look of amusement, even today. While in his fifties, his youthful countenance belied his age. One had to look closely to see the grey streaks in his golden hair.

"Can a man not bathe in peace?"

"Not when that man is the subject of a scandal set to bring Worthen to his knees." Tregarth snatched the meerschaum from Benedict's fingers, put his mouth to the pipe and drew in the tobacco smoke. "Hmm. While it relaxes the mind, it does nothing to calm the soul. You have that tortured look about you, the one I've not seen for years."

Benedict instructed Perkins to pour two glasses of wine and then dismissed the footman. "News spreads quickly."

"Gossip is the *ton*'s favourite pastime." His father continued to puff on the pipe, blowing smoke high into the air in the same languid fashion he did most things. "And when a devil gets his comeuppance, his enemies like to rejoice."

There was no need to berate his father, to remind him a woman had lost her dignity. Or that her reputation was as soiled as the chemise that had covered her modesty. Tregarth merely voiced the opinion of the masses.

"And yet it's not the devil who will pay the price."

"No," Tregarth mused, handing Benedict the pipe and snatching his wine goblet from the trestle table. "After they've stopped dancing on Worthen's grave, people will pity the girl and blame the reckless rake who sought to take advantage." Tregarth spoke of the fool who'd cradled a semi-naked woman in his arms amongst a host of witnesses.

"Then perhaps I should work to prove my innocence.

Perhaps I should focus my efforts on finding the rogue who kidnapped Cassandra Mills from Lord Craven's ball and dumped her in the park." Benedict drew on the pipe to banish all thoughts of what a blackguard would do to a drugged woman.

"Can anyone vouch for your whereabouts last night?" Tregarth sipped his wine while studying Benedict over the rim of his glass, concern the overriding emotion, not suspicion.

"I spent the evening in Bruton Street dining with the Wycliffs, Trent and Miss Vale." A memorable evening dominated by talk of love and marriage and the happiness that came when a man found solace in a life companion. They had laughed about Mrs Crandall's obsession, reassured him that he, too, would find the one person who was his match in every way, oblivious to his real thoughts and feelings on the matter. "I left early, returned home at eleven. The letter arrived shortly after midnight."

"The letter telling you to visit the Serpentine at dawn?"

"Indeed."

"You're a man with a strong mind, a man who rarely does what he's told." Admiration clung to his father's words. "You witness shocking sights at every demimonde rout and soirée. What drew you out of bed at such an ungodly hour?"

Benedict placed his pipe on the table. He captured his goblet and took to savouring the taste of the expensive claret while contemplating the question.

"It had nothing to do with the persuasive tone," he said, "and everything to do with a strange feeling in my gut." Not strange—compelling. "Evidently, the sender assigned me a role in this farce, and I took to the stage as if I were born to act."

Tregarth remained silent for a time. "Whoever did this to you will pay dearly."

Benedict snorted. "I'm strong enough to deal with anything thrown my way. Lady Cassandra is the one who deserves justice." And he would occupy his mind by finding the person responsible.

"After all these years, after the despicable way she treated you, your thoughts turn to her welfare."

"All men have an Achilles heel." And Cassandra Mills was his.

"And so what will you do now that Lord Murray has freed himself from his obligation?"

It took a moment for the news to penetrate Benedict's brain. "Murray has done what!" Benedict sat up so fast water splashed onto the boards. Despite the warm water his blood ran cold. "The spineless bastard."

"You cannot blame Murray. When a man engages in a business transaction, he must approach matters from a logical perspective."

Nausea roiled in Benedict's stomach. Indeed, he could almost feel Cassandra's wrenching despair. "The lady made a mistake when she chose Murray and must live with the consequences. Worthen will find someone for her to wed." Even at that, she would be barred from respectable events. "And I shall bear the daggers of disdain just as I have done my whole life."

The twitch of his father's cheek was the only visible sign of the guilt he bore. The flash of pride in his eyes spoke of the love and loyalty that eased the burden of Benedict's illegitimacy.

A knock on the door brought Perkins. The footman inclined his head—an apology for the intrusion—and announced that the Earl of Worthen and Lady Cassandra Mills were waiting in the drawing room.

Shock rendered Benedict momentarily speechless.

Tregarth pulled his watch from his pocket and angled the face towards the candlelight. "It's almost nine o'clock." A smug grin formed on his father's lips. "For Worthen to call at this late hour, he must have something important to say."

"Do you know something I don't?"

"Not at all, yet one cannot help but feel some satisfaction when his enemy accepts defeat."

"Defeat? I imagine Worthen has come to accuse me of kidnapping and ravishment."

"I wouldn't be so sure."

Perkins cleared his throat. "Shall I tell them you're indisposed, sir?"

The last thing Benedict wanted was another confrontation with the earl. Trent and Verity were marrying at St George's in the morning, and after the scandal in Hyde Park, he needed his wits to cope with their outpouring of love.

"Tell them I have no desire—"

"No," Tregarth interjected. "The intuitive feeling that saw you ride to Hyde Park at dawn tells me you should dress and meet your guests in the drawing room."

"The urge to turn Worthen away overrules all other sensations." And the warm water had eased his pain a little. Why would he let them take turns hurling insults? "The lord seeks every opportunity to cast aspersions on my character. I'll not listen to his vile diatribe whilst in my own home."

Tregarth arched a brow. "You can always throw Worthen out. And you cannot miss an opportunity to watch him squirm in discomfort. Surely you're intrigued to know what he wants."

Benedict sighed. Sparks of curiosity fired to life in his brain. Perhaps the earl had found the culprit and had come to make an apology. Perhaps the villain had concocted lies to incriminate the fool who'd been first to arrive at Hyde Park.

"If I'm to meet them, I shall do so on my own terms." When his father frowned, Benedict added, "They think I'm a scandalous rogue and so a scandalous rogue is what they will get."

Benedict kept the earl and Cassandra waiting for twenty minutes while he swallowed two glasses of claret and threw on his breeches and shirt. He mussed his damp hair. He didn't bother with shoes or boots, a waistcoat or cravat and decided to let his shirt flap open, revealing his bare chest.

"You should wear boots," Tregarth said, observing Benedict's relaxed attire. "Bare feet suggests a certain submissiveness as opposed to a man who cares nothing for propriety."

Feeling exposed without footwear, he took his father's advice.

Benedict entered the drawing room to find the earl pacing, wringing his hands in frustration. Cassandra sat demurely in the chair flanking the hearth, her tired eyes and sullen face framed in a pretty poke bonnet. A fashionable cornflower blue pelisse and lemon kid gloves hid her bruises and scratches.

"About time." Worthen blinked back his shock when he noted Benedict's flagrant dishabille. He puffed out his chest in outrage and glared at his daughter. "Did I not tell you the shameless rogue was upstairs writhing with his mistress while we're left waiting down here?"

"A rogue has no need of a mistress." Benedict brushed his hand through his damp hair, aware of Cassandra's intense gaze fixed on the opening of his shirt. "A rogue enjoys the freedom to bed any woman he chooses."

Worthen sucked in a sharp breath. "This … this heathen isn't worthy of our time or our regard." His jowls wobbled as he shook his head. "His tainted blood makes him unfit for those in polite society."

"Then leave." Benedict gestured to the door. "As you say, I have more important matters that require my attention."

Again, Worthen turned on Cassandra. "See, he doesn't want you. He made that perfectly clear this morning. In your weak state, you're allowing sentiment to cloud your mind."

"Surprisingly, my head is clearer than it has been in years." Cassandra's confident voice supported her claim. She seemed different. Whoever had stripped her of her clothes and reputation had stripped away her arrogance, too. And she no longer sat rigid with fear in Worthen's presence, no longer winced when the stern lord barked his commands. “Why would Mr Cavanagh want me when I have behaved so abominably?”

Shock stole the air from his lungs.

It was the first time Cassandra had admitted to her failings. Yet, regardless of how she behaved, a small part of him would always want the young woman he once knew. But surely they had not come expecting him to propose marriage. Worthen despised every bone in his body.

Benedict mentally checked the invisible suit of steel he wore to protect him from their endless taunts. The next few minutes would be unpleasant, to say the least.

“Why would I want you,” he agreed, “when you’re betrothed to Lord Murray, and you have already made it clear my lineage is lacking?” He couldn’t wait to hear Worthen explain that his beloved baron had failed to step up to the mark.

But it was Cassandra who spoke. “Timothy cannot marry a woman with a soiled reputation. His mother would never allow him to commit social suicide.”

“Then Murray doesn’t know a thing about love.”

“His love came with conditions,” she agreed with an air of indifference despite the fact her red-rimmed eyes bore the evidence of shed tears. “In the face of adversity, some people lack the heart to stand by their convictions.”

“Well, you would know.”

She took the verbal hit with equanimity. “Those who sow inconstancy reap it. Is that not how people learn and grow?”

“Education is all well and good as long as no one is hurt in the process.”

“Cease with this nonsense,” Worthen interjected. “I’ve heard enough pathetic talk to last a lifetime. Do you want to marry my daughter or not?”

“No.”

The earl looked flabbergasted. His cheeks ballooned. His eyes bulged, and he gasped like a fish out of water. “I told her all efforts to plead to your sense of honour were futile.”

Cassandra hung her head. It took a moment for her to gather her composure, and she rose gracefully to her feet. She closed the gap between them, captured Benedict's hand and stared deep into his eyes.

"Where you're concerned, I don't deserve a second chance." A sad sigh left her lips, though his body struggled to cope with the sudden surge of awareness that always accompanied close contact. "And you're right to refuse. Had Timothy kept his oath, I would have married him and pushed all memories of the past aside." Water welled in her eyes, and she swallowed hard. "Thank you for your assistance this morning. We shall leave you to attend to your guest."

She released his hand, and he almost groaned at the loss. But he could not trust her motives, couldn't trust her word. He could not live with seeing her every day, couldn't risk joining her in bed. And yet his thoughts turned to her welfare. The earl must have exhausted every other suitor. Benedict must be her last hope. What would she do now? It shouldn't matter to him. But it did.

"You would marry me, knowing I am entertaining someone else upstairs?" Someone who just happened to be his father. "You would be happy knowing I bed other women?"

A pained expression marred her fine features. "You know the answer, Benedict, but I am not in a position to make demands."

"The blighter is punishing you. Can you not see that?" Worthen just couldn't keep his damn mouth shut. "Numerous gentlemen will have you. Tomorrow I shall visit Chadderton. You won't have to bow and scrape to him."

"Chadderton? The man is sixty years of age." The thought of the old devil's bony fingers roaming over Cassandra's soft skin made Benedict mentally retch.

"There's Lord Theakston," Worthen countered. "He has always admired her. And Viscount Barton's youngest son."

Confusion sought to muddle Benedict's senses. Was he not

their last hope? He glared at the earl. "And you did not think to visit those gentlemen before coming here?"

"The harrowing events of the day have turned my daughter into a bumbling buffoon."

Another resigned sigh escaped Cassandra's lips. "Benedict, I will marry you or I will marry no one. My father can throw me into the gutter for all I care, but I will not be a pawn in his power game."

Worthen muttered a string of obscenities beneath his breath.

It took Benedict every effort to suppress the surge of joy that would have him bend the knee and pretend the last five years never existed. Bitterness surfaced. She had ruined his life once before and was set to ruin it again. Still, the prospect of having her at his beck and call proved as tempting as the forbidden fruit.

"My dowry is substantial enough that I would not be a financial burden."

"Your dowry is unacceptable." Pride would see him refuse every penny the earl offered.

"Now, listen here. If you think to use this scandal to bleed me dry, you can think again," Worthen snapped.

Benedict ignored the earl's tantrum. "If I marry your daughter, I'll marry her without a dowry. I don't need your money, and I don't need your condescension. I shall set aside a portion of equal value to be used for settlements and security for her and future children and have legal documents drawn to protect her interests."

Cassandra's eyes widened in disbelief. "What are you saying? That you will marry me?"

In his need to challenge the earl, his imagination had run wild.

Benedict paused for a moment. Would possessing the one thing denied him ease the infernal pain? With Trent marrying, what would he do with his time? Indeed, the parties, the wild carousing, the scandalous goings-on in the demimonde had lost their appeal. And he could not imagine loving a woman the way he once loved Cassandra.

"You have yet to propose," he said, relishing the look of shock on the lady's face.

"Me? You want me to beg, to get down on bended knee?"

Worthen continued to mumble incoherent nonsense.

"I don't want you to beg, Cassandra, but you will give me three reasons why you want me for your husband." He would know if she lied, if she spouted sentiment to appease him. And while they could live separate lives despite being married, it would be better to start on a positive note.

"I lost my reputation, my dignity, and you would still make me suffer?"

"I doubt I shall ever trust you again. Give me some truth if I'm to gamble everything on making you my wife." He turned to the earl. He would not have the cruel lord party to their intimate conversation. "Wait in the carriage. This will take but a moment."

The earl was about to protest when Cassandra said, "No doubt you're the reason I stand here with no option but to bare my soul. At least have the decency to afford me some privacy."

Tregarth appeared in the doorway. "You heard what your daughter said, George. Indeed, I shall join you in the cramped confines as I, too, have a few things to say."

Worthen sneered. "I should have known you were here. What is this? A family orgy?"

"The carriage, George," Tregarth reinforced in a steely voice sure to frighten most men. "Else I shall drag you there myself. If our children decide to marry, we will have to argue the case with the archbishop. Better you air your grievances with me first."

After a tense few seconds, Worthen obliged.

Left alone, Benedict studied Cassandra. The last time she'd looked so nervous, he'd been about to press his lips to hers—the first kiss of many. "I'm sorry Lord Murray proved false-hearted. I know what it's like to have the rug ripped from under your feet, leaving you staggering and wondering how you'll ever stand straight."

"Yes."

"Well?" He paused. "Three reasons, Cassandra. Three honest reasons. You owe me that."

"Yes." She shuffled awkwardly on the spot, wrung her hands and struggled to calm her erratic breathing. Eventually, she said, "When life drags you through the dirt, you need to know there are people you may depend upon. Today, you proved to be the only trustworthy gentleman of my acquaintance."

"A trustworthy gentleman?" He was impressed. "Not the spurious son of a philanderer?" She had called him that on many occasions.

"A gentleman." She nodded. "I saw a strength in you I have never seen before."

"Is that the second reason?"

"No." She lifted her chin. "I would like to marry you because an undeniable connection exists between us." She bit down on her bottom lip as her gaze dipped to the opening of his shirt. "I've felt it my whole life."

"A connection so undeniable you cast me aside," he mocked.

"I cannot undo the past, Benedict. You wanted a reason, and I have given you one."

This lady was as dangerous as he feared. Already, his heart thumped faster, and the warmth in his chest took to journeying southward. "And the third reason?"

"To reveal the third would leave me more exposed than when you found me in Hyde Park. Soon, when I am strong again, I will confide in you. For now, my third reason must be that I admire the fact nothing fazes you. You walk tall despite every wicked accusation I have hurled your way."

And there had been many.

"Tregarth once told me that a man should not be ashamed of situations beyond his control. Equally, when people push a man to the outskirts of society, no one can blame him for making his life there."

Silence descended.

Cassandra shuffled nervously. "Now you have heard my reasons you must tell me your answer."

His whole life—his future happiness—hung on this one decision. He wasn't sure how they would survive the lies, the deceit, how they would live in the aftermath of their bitter war. Still, he gave the only answer he could under the circumstances. The only answer his heart would allow.

"Yes, Cassandra. I will marry you."

CHAPTER FIVE

When Lady Cassandra Mills married in St George's it would be the most elaborate wedding of the year, the decade. With her mask in place, she would walk gracefully down the aisle in a dress designed exclusively by Madame de La Tour and show the world that power and position mattered more than truth and love. The aristocracy were too intelligent to live life from the heart. One only had to glance around Mayfair to know that strength came from a healthy bank balance and the right connections.

During the last five years she had worked tirelessly, convincing herself that real ladies made sacrifices. Blue bloods had a responsibility that went beyond the realms of lesser mortals. And so, in the process of pretending, she had lost herself. She had become a mere pawn in a game, a piece her parent had surrendered for the greater good.

But now, as she stood opposite Benedict Cavanagh in her father's drawing room in Cavendish Square, a mere two days since the tragic event that changed her life, she had never been more terrified.

The joining of two people should be a happy affair, and yet practically every person in the room despised her. The Earl of

Tregarth did not look at her once but kept his intense gaze focused on his beloved son. Mr Damian Wycliff and Mr Lawrence Trent watched the proceedings with solemn faces, shaking their heads when Benedict agreed to take her for his wife. The men's wives dabbed their eyes and sniffed as if attending a wake, not a wedding.

The three people there to offer her support—her father and her friends Miss Sybil Atwood and Miss Rosamund Fox, the latter having arrived late—looked on with faces marred with shock, denial and a good dose of pity.

And then there was Benedict.

He looked so handsome in his dark blue coat. The diamond pin in his cravat conveyed the sparkle missing from his eyes. Many times, she had lain awake at night and imagined marrying him. A romantic union under an arbour of white and pink roses. A time of smiles and gaiety. But there were no flowers today, no smiles, no laughter—just two people converging onto a road that was sure to lead to disaster.

The last few minutes of the service passed by in a blur. Only when Benedict placed a guiding hand at her back and steered her towards their guests did the gravity of what they'd done hit her. How did one salvage something from a wreckage ravaged by harsh words, battered by the cruel hand of fate?

"You declined Worthen's offer of a wedding breakfast?" Mr Wycliff placed his hand on Benedict's shoulder—a gesture of support and friendship. "There's to be no celebration?"

Benedict's downturned mouth reflected everyone's sullen mood. "Tregarth and Worthen cannot tolerate each other's company. We will return to Jermyn Street, though expect the announcement will cause another bitter row."

"My father insists we live here until we find a more suitable place to reside." Cassandra's stomach roiled with nerves. His friends would never approve of her, but she could not remain silent her entire life. "Benedict refused, but my father struggles to accept other people's opinions."

Oh, Lord! Her chest was so tight she thought she might swoon.

"Cavanagh is your husband," snapped Mr Trent, offering his usual brooding stare. "The decision is his as to where you live. Jermyn Street is a perfectly acceptable location."

"I couldn't agree more." Cassandra forced a smile.

An uncomfortable silence ensued.

No doubt there were a host of things Mr Wycliff and Mr Trent wanted to say. Indeed, she almost wished they would as it might help to banish the tension in the air.

"I know you all think I am a terrible person," she said, unable to cope with the oppressive silence a moment longer. "All I ask is that you do not judge me on past mistakes but give me a chance to show I can be a good wife to Benedict."

It was Mrs Wycliff who reached out to her, who touched her gently on the arm and said, "None of us stand here as perfect exemplars of appropriate behaviour. I have made some dreadful decisions, some painful mistakes. We care about Benedict and cannot help but have grave concerns for his welfare."

"There is no need to worry on my account. I'm sure we can all be friends," Benedict said though his tone lacked conviction. "Given time."

"Speaking of friends, I should thank mine for risking society's wrath by attending today." And it would give her another chance to probe them about the events surrounding Lord Craven's ball. "If you'll excuse me." Suppressing a sigh of relief, Cassandra took her leave.

"Oh, I'm sorry I arrived late." Rosamund rushed to clasp Cassandra's hands in a show of solidarity. "It was so difficult to slip away." The beauty's brown curls bobbed, and her green eyes begged for forgiveness. "If my aunt knew I was here, she'd have me transported to the country."

"For keeping company with a shameless harlot?" Cassandra joked, but her friend's cheeks flamed, and her gaze dropped to her boots. "That is what they call me now?"

Rosamund nodded. "The gossip making the rounds is vicious. People are saying terrible things."

So, the comments were as vile as she imagined.

Nausea came upon her again.

"Pay it no heed, Cassandra." Sybil cast Rosamund a look of reproach. "It's your wedding day. Myopia is a disease common throughout the *ton*, and I'm afraid there is no cure."

"Yes," Rosamund said weakly. "I'm sure people will forget all about it in a year or two. Of course, it means you will miss Lady Casterberry's ball, and Lady Forrester's soirée held in support of Lord Forrester's patronage of the arts."

After the incident in the park, Cassandra hoped never to see Lord Forrester again. "Thank you for reminding me I am a social pariah."

Rosamund blushed. "Forgive me. I'm utterly useless when dealing with those plagued by scandal. No doubt your social calendar will alter somewhat. They say Mr Cavanagh attends many of the demimonde's disreputable functions. You will, too."

Cassandra had heard about Benedict's wild antics from her father. "The demimonde's gatherings will be a welcome change. Besides, terrible things happen in respectable places. I am living proof of that." She had already written to both ladies begging for information about that fateful night only to receive vague replies, but it wouldn't hurt to press them both again now. "Have either of you remembered anything about what happened before you noticed I was missing?"

Sybil shook her head. "You asked me to watch your father in the card room and to let you know once he'd finished play."

"You looked a little peaky," Rosamund said, "but insisted on visiting the ladies' retiring room alone. I assumed you were merely suffering from nerves and intended to sneak out into the garden to meet Lord Murray. We would have raised the alarm had we known of your predicament."

A depressing silence descended.

"Despite your reluctance to marry," Sybil said, "might I say you look beautiful today. Your complexion is positively glowing, and your dress is divine. Peacock blue is perfect for you."

Sybil cared little for superficial things, which made her comments more endearing. She was more bluestocking than a diamond of the first water. Indeed, they might never have been friends had the earl not forced the issue for his own selfish gain.

Rosamund's eyes widened, and she gasped. "Good Lord. Mr Cavanagh is looking directly at us. Do you think he might come over?" The lady sounded panicked. She stared at Benedict and his friends as if they were otherworldly beings. Monsters set to rip out the hearts of godly folk.

"Rosamund, you should assess a person's character after making their acquaintance." Sybil sighed. "Not make assumptions based on gossip."

"Not all gossip is fabricated nonsense." Rosamund's bottom lip quivered. "Oh, Lord, he's coming over. What do I say?"

Sybil clicked her tongue. "You could offer your felicitations."

"But neither of them wanted to marry."

That was untrue. Cassandra had always wanted to marry Benedict Cavanagh.

"Still, it is the polite thing to say."

"Nothing you could say would upset or faze him," Cassandra said as the most handsome man ever to make her acquaintance strode over to stand at her side. She straightened her spine and smiled. "Benedict, may I introduce my friends, Miss Rosamund Fox and Miss Sybil Atwood."

"A pleasure." Benedict bowed.

Rosamund looked terrified, as if he might devour her with razor-sharp fangs. Clearly she wasn't sure if one curtsied to a god of the underworld and, somewhat awkwardly, followed Sybil's lead when she dipped a curtsy as a mark of respect.

"Sir William Fox's daughter?" Benedict asked with a hint of suspicion. Surely he didn't think her friends had anything to do with what happened in the park. "I have made your father's acquaintance many times."

As Benedict rarely attended society functions, he must have met Sir William at the demimonde's soirées, but Rosamund said somewhat naively, "Oh! Do you have an interest in the mining industry, too, Mr Cavanagh?"

A mischievous smile played on her husband's lips. "Delving into cramped, dark places is not my forte, Miss Fox, though your father approaches the business with such vigorous passion."

"My father takes his investments seriously, sir."

"Indeed."

"May I offer my congratulations, Mr Cavanagh?" Sybil did not cower before the scandalous son of Lord Tregarth but looked him keenly in the eye. "If anyone possesses the wherewithal to assist Cassandra through this scandal, it is you, sir."

"Do I sense a compliment there, Miss Atwood?" Benedict teased as he scanned the lady's vibrant red hair and emerald green pelisse.

"You do, sir. While I have limited experience of the male character, any man who rises above society's hypocritical dictates deserves respect."

"As a man known to speak bluntly, Miss Atwood, I am surprised Lord Worthen permitted his daughter to associate with a lady who boasts of such original ideas."

There it was again, that air of distrust and suspicion.

"But then you are the daughter of Mr Atticus Atwood, are you not?" Benedict continued. "A man renowned and often castigated for his modern views."

Cassandra blinked back her surprise. Did Benedict know everything about everyone in the *ton*?

Sybil smiled. "My father died almost a year ago, but yes, he was a most remarkable man. A man whose foresight left me with the means to make my own choices."

"An enviable position for any lady."

The sound of raised voices drew everyone's attention to the

hall. Through the closed study door, it wasn't difficult to identify the two powerful voices embroiled in an argument.

"You'd do anything to boost your son's position. You orchestrated this whole damn thing to punish me for renouncing our friendship. You know how weak Cassandra is when it comes to your wretched son."

So weak, she had spent five years punishing Benedict for her own stupid failings.

One of their parents punched something hollow.

"Must you hurl your pathetic accusations on their wedding day?"

"The marriage is a sham."

"They loved each other once," Lord Tregarth countered. "And if I discover one of your enemies used them as a means for vengeance there'll be hell to pay."

"Miss Fox, Miss Atwood, we thank you both for coming," Benedict said, struggling to maintain eye contact as his gaze drifted back to the study door. "You're both welcome to visit my wife in Jermyn Street should she desire your company."

No doubt he knew neither of her friends could be seen in the home of a well-known scoundrel. "Or perhaps we might take a trip to New Bond Street or visit Gunters," Cassandra said, forcing a smile despite the fracas in the study.

While Sybil agreed, Rosamund clearly struggled with the idea of being seen with a woman who'd brought such a dreadful scandal to town. Cassandra couldn't blame her. When one had an overbearing parent, it was impossible to think for oneself.

Benedict glanced over his shoulder. He spoke briefly to his friends and arranged to visit Mr Wycliff on the morrow. His friends took it as their cue to depart. Rosamund and Sybil followed closely behind.

"Are you ready to leave?" Benedict asked. Anger radiated from every aspect of his being. "I'll not stay in this house a moment longer."

"Suspecting my father would make a fuss, I had the footman

load my luggage into your carriage shortly after you arrived." Nothing would stop her leaving with Benedict today.

A look of admiration and camaraderie passed between them. "Then fetch your pelisse and meet me outside."

She didn't need to ask what he intended to do. He marched towards the study like Satan's servant ready to unleash fire, brimstone and eternal damnation on the two unsuspecting occupants. Cassandra hurried into the hall as Benedict burst into the study, almost taking the door off its hinges.

"How dare you!" he roared. "How dare you humiliate my wife on our wedding day. Everyone heard your vile diatribe. Tregarth should have put you on your arse long ago. But I swear, do anything to ridicule her again, speak distastefully of our marriage, and I shall have no qualms in beating you to a bloody pulp."

Awestruck, Cassandra stood and watched her husband berate her father. If only he'd spoken with such courage and determination years ago. How different their lives might have been.

Benedict did not wait for a response. He marched towards her, captured her hand and drew her to the front door. "Forget your pelisse. Buy a new one. Buy whatever you need."

They sat in silence as the carriage covered the mile journey to Jermyn Street. To Benedict's home. The place where he had thrown wild parties and entertained his demimonde friends. Anxiety reared its head again. They were from different worlds. They were more different now than ever before. It was as if they stood on opposite sides of a river bank, resentment flowing between them.

Anger still infused his tone when he introduced her to his servants—their servants now. And while they greeted her with the polite respectfulness expected, she wondered what scandalous things they had witnessed during their service. What did the staff really think of their master?

"I live modestly here," Benedict said, his body stiff and tense as he escorted her upstairs. "Meet with Mrs Rampling and make whatever changes you feel appropriate. Hire more staff if you think it necessary. You're free to do as you please. I'm not a power-hungry lord who gets pleasure from controlling his wife."

Anger, she could tolerate. This coldness, this distance he placed between them, left a cavernous hole in her heart. It was as if they were strangers forced to cohabit. The more he spoke, the more the crippling sense of loneliness took hold. She was wrong to expect anything else, but if they were ever to find happiness they had mountains to climb.

"I prefer to discuss any suggestions with you and come to a mutual decision." She swallowed down her nerves as he directed her to a bedchamber left of the landing. "Perhaps we might set aside some time each day for important discussions." A time where they might work to heal the wounds of the past.

Suspicion flashed in his eyes as he cast her a sidelong glance. "We shall dine together each evening. That should afford time to deal with household matters."

Her resolve almost cracked at his icy reply. It shattered into a million pieces when he led her into the bedchamber and she realised she would be sleeping there alone.

"The same applies here," he said, gesturing to the room decorated in sage green. "Speak to Mrs Rampling about ordering new curtains. Perhaps you would prefer a more feminine scheme. There's an escritoire in another chamber. Have a footman move it in here should you wish a private place to attend to your correspondence."

Why would she need privacy? What would she have to hide from her husband? Surely he didn't mean for her to seek affection outside of their marriage, write secrets notes to a lover?

"Strange," she said, laughing lightly else she might cry, "I took you for a man who slept in the same bed as his wife." She remembered the passionate embraces, the soul-deep kisses that curled her toes.

His head shot in her direction. "When I'm in love with a woman, I give everything of myself. You know that."

"And when you're not, you prefer to maintain a certain distance."

"Indeed."

Was she the only person who'd hurt him? Had there been someone else he'd cared for just as deeply? "Have you loved anyone else since me?" She regretted asking almost immediately.

His Adam's apple bobbed in his throat, and he swallowed numerous times. "No. No one else. I'm wiser now than I was then."

"I'm sorry." She wanted to reveal all the loving words buried deep in her heart, but she had locked them away, secured by so many iron chains she wouldn't know how to unravel them. "Sorry for everything that happened between us."

"Pay it no mind. It's unhealthy to live in the past."

A tense silence descended.

He inclined his head and moved towards the door.

"Wait!" Her tone rang of an inner desperation. "I never thought I would ask such a blatant question, but … but do you intend to come to my room tonight?" While the thought of joining him in bed set her body aflame, she couldn't love him knowing he didn't want her.

"It's unwise to complicate matters further." A pained expression marred his face. "Cassandra, I have no notion how we will move forward, how we might nurture a friendship let alone deal with anything more profound."

The man was a walking conundrum. His words and gestures were sometimes contradictory. He could protect her when others attacked but couldn't love her. And yet she had untold respect for his wisdom in this time of uncertainty.

"Perhaps there is a way forward," she said, knowing they had to find a distraction. "I want to find out who drugged me and played God with my life. I want to punish the person who used you to achieve his goal, the person who forced you to partake in this debacle."

He pondered her comment for a moment. "Vengeance is a dangerous game." The devilish glint in his eyes said she had piqued his interest. "Are you prepared for what we might discover?"

She couldn't help but cast a sly smile. "After what I've experienced these last few days, I'm prepared for anything."

"Then you must suspect everyone—family, your closest friends and allies—until we work to prove their innocence. It will not be easy. Those doors once open to you will be barred."

"There must be a way to discover the truth. Someone must have seen or heard something."

"Knowledge is power. There are people within the demimonde willing to sell the *ton*'s secrets for the right price."

Cassandra breathed a silent sigh. The conversation flowed freely again. Gone were the strained looks and awkward glances. In their bid to discover the truth, they shared a common ground and so what better place to start rebuilding their relationship.

"I'm willing to do whatever it takes."

Benedict pursed his lips. "You must tell me everything about that night. Everything you remember. The most insignificant thing might be an important clue. We will begin tomorrow. Take today to become familiar with the house. We will dine together, and then I must go out for a few hours."

"You're going out tonight?" Jealousy wrapped around her heart like a strangling vine. "You have an engagement that cannot be postponed, not even on your wedding day?"

Benedict shuffled uncomfortably. He opened his mouth to speak but then shook his head and said, "I could lie and make an excuse, but you're right. Nothing should be more important than two people in love sharing their first evening as man and wife. But that's not what this is. And I'm unsure as to how I might survive the night knowing we're sleeping under the same roof."

Well, she could not accuse him of dishonesty.

Benedict Cavanagh did not make promises he couldn't keep.

"Then do what you must." She only hoped his need to

occupy his mind didn't send him racing back to the demi-monde's hellish pit. "I'm eternally grateful for everything you've done for me, and tomorrow we will make a start on our investigation."

He inclined his head and then left her alone.

The isolation made her feel small and insignificant, made the room seem suddenly vast. But she had to take heart. Had to remain optimistic. It was always darkest before the dawn of a new day.

CHAPTER SIX

"Hell! You look like you're the one who spent the night sleeping in the park." Damian Wycliff ushered Benedict into the drawing room and gestured for him to take a seat on the sofa. "I know you rarely drink at this hour of the morning but judging by the dark circles framing your eyes I'm tempted to offer you brandy."

Benedict had spent the night circling Hyde Park in his carriage, walking the length and breadth of the Serpentine, assessing how someone had transported an unconscious woman without being seen. Of course, avoiding his bride was the main reason for his midnight escapade.

"A large glass of brandy will be most welcome considering I've had but a few hours' sleep."

"Wild night?" Wycliff cast a sinful grin as he pulled the crystal top from the decanter. "They say love and hate are opposite sides of the same coin. Judging by your bleary eyes, I presume your wife had no issue testing the theory."

"Not when a bitter heart is a disease from which one rarely recovers." Benedict knew the moment Wycliff crossed the room and handed him the glass that his friend would read something of the truth on his face.

"She rejected your advances?" Wycliff narrowed his gaze in a look of suspicion. "Then you stand by your earlier statement. You intend to live separate lives and have married purely for convenience."

"There is nothing convenient about taking a wife." Just knowing Cassandra was in the same house unsettled his equilibrium. "Doubtless it takes time to adjust."

Wycliff dropped into the chair opposite and continued his visual scrutiny. A light of recognition flashed in his dark eyes. "Devil take it, tell me you didn't seek revenge for her snub and take your pleasure elsewhere."

Benedict remained silent, trying to find the right words to explain that it wasn't his wife who was unwilling.

"Good God, you've been married a day. Tell me you've not taken a mistress out of spite." Wycliff sat forward. "I know it must be difficult watching your friends fall in love but be patient. You loved each other once and might come to share a mutual affection again."

"Of course I haven't taken a mistress. Credit me with some morals." In all fairness, when he'd first told Wycliff of his impending marriage to Cassandra Mills, he had said she was free to take a lover. It was a foolish comment said purely as a means of self-preservation. "I intend to be faithful to my wife."

"Even though she takes great pleasure in humiliating you? I fear she will continue to reject your advances merely as a means of revenge."

The need to defend Cassandra burst to life in Benedict's chest. He would not give his friends further reason to dislike her. "Cassandra did not reject my advances. I'm the one who refused the possibility of an amorous liaison."

Wycliff jerked his head back. He looked at Benedict through incredulous eyes. "Did you get the impression she wanted you to bed her?"

"She seemed receptive to the idea, yes, but I'll not have relations with a woman because she wishes to express her gratitude."

Wycliff appeared more confused than ever.

Benedict sighed with frustration. How the devil could he make Wycliff understand? "A man should make love to his wife, not tumble her like Haymarket ware. When resentment clouds one's judgement, it is possible to confuse the two."

Wycliff's eyes widened. "Good God." He relaxed back in the chair and laughed. "You're still in love with her. That's why you married her. That's why you've taken the risk. It makes more sense now.

"I'm not in love with her, but remnants of the old feelings are always there. We've despised each other for so long I'm not certain what is real anymore."

"Does Tregarth know this is how you feel?"

"Before you jump to conclusions, my father did not arrange Cassandra's ruination so that I might marry her." Tregarth would do anything to secure Benedict's happiness, but he would never stoop to such vile tactics. "Nor would he hurt an innocent to punish Lord Worthen."

Wycliff steepled his fingers and offered a mischievous grin. "Then we should strike him off the list of suspects."

"List of suspects? How do you know I am out for revenge?" Oh, he was out to punish someone for treating his wife so despicably.

"Well, if you weren't out all night bedding women to banish thoughts of your wife, you must have been doing something to occupy your mind. Indeed, I took the liberty of visiting my father last night and made some enquiries of my own."

Benedict drained the tumbler of brandy and put the empty glass on the side table. "Did you discover anything of interest?"

"The most notable members of the *ton* attended Lord Craven's ball, including my father. By all accounts, Lord Purcell has a vendetta against Worthen and has slandered the earl's name all over town."

"A vendetta?" It came as no surprise. Most people despised the earl. "Then it's no coincidence he was one of the men who received a note to come to Hyde Park." Of course, Purcell might have written the notes himself, arranged the whole damn thing knowing Benedict was the last person Worthen wanted his daughter to marry. "Does your father know what started the feud?"

"There was a bankruptcy auction for Reavey Hall, a substantial property in Shropshire which borders Purcell's estate. Tenders were submitted as sealed bids, but Purcell believes Worthen filed more than one bid and bribed a clerk to present the appropriate one. There's no proof, but Worthen ridiculed Purcell for lacking the funds to make a serious offer."

Benedict absorbed the information. Lord Worthen loved nothing more than belittling men he deemed inferior. Purcell was guilty of the same, so it was no surprise the men were embroiled in a bitter dispute.

"So Purcell has a motive. What about opportunity?"

Wycliff arched a brow. "That's where it gets interesting. Trent went to Lord Craven's mews and bribed a groom. On the night in question, a man fitting Purcell's description bungled a woman with blonde hair into his carriage. The vehicle bolted from the mews as if the wheels were ablaze."

Benedict jumped to his feet. "By God, then Purcell is the villain responsible." And he would fire a lead ball between the lord's brows for his treachery. "Only a man could have carried Cassandra's body from the road to the Serpentine."

"It pays not to jump to conclusions. The groom said numerous drunken couples climbed into their carriages that night. Does Cassandra recall speaking to Purcell at the ball? You said someone drugged her, so she must have encountered her kidnapper."

Benedict dropped into the seat. He'd been so desperate to place some distance between them he'd not taken the time to question Cassandra. "We agreed to make a detailed account of events during dinner tonight. Her memory is so hazy I saw no reason to distress her by pressing for information."

Wycliff nodded, which went some way to easing Benedict's embarrassment. "There's something else you should know. I met with Woods last night, too."

"Mrs Crandall's majordomo? What, has he finally escaped her evil clutches?" Besides greeting guests and serving drinks, Mrs Crandall's servant often performed private services for his mistress.

"Woods is trying to gather enough funds to make a new life for himself in Boston. I paid him handsomely for the information last night, though he asked me to remind you that if you intend to travel abroad, he would happily act as your valet."

"The man is so desperate to leave Mrs Crandall's employ I might pay for his fare myself." Benedict knew firsthand what it was like to be the recipient of the woman's rampant affections.

"Trent said the same." Wycliff gestured to the row of decanters on the drinks table. "Another brandy?"

"Not for me. When I return home, I'd rather not smell as if I've partaken in a night of drunken debauchery." Cassandra had taken her breakfast in her room this morning, and so had no idea what time he had come home. "What did Woods say?"

"That Mrs Crandall is as obsessed with you as ever. Drummond, McCreath and Forrester have never been to her den of vice on Theobolds Road. Purcell visited last week, took tea in the drawing room, and Woods swears Purcell mentioned Lord Worthen's name."

Benedict fell silent. How would ruining Cassandra help Mrs Crandall's bid to win his affections? "Mrs Crandall has nothing to gain by hurting Lord Worthen. Perhaps she discovered how much I despise Cassandra and gave me her ruination as a gift." That was one of many scenarios he'd considered after arriving in Hyde Park.

"Then she will be livid when she learns you married the lady."

Jealousy and vindictiveness pulsed in the madam's veins. If Mrs Crandall had played a part in the scandal, then she was likely to find other ways to hurt Cassandra. Panic burst to life in Benedict's chest. Until the matter was resolved, he should not let his wife out of his sight.

"I should return to Jermyn Street." Perhaps he was exaggerating the threat. But someone had gone to great lengths to cause a scandal. Without knowing the villain's motive, it was impossible to predict his next move. "While I'm confident the aim was to ridicule the Earl of Worthen, what if the culprit is intent on punishing Cassandra?"

"Your objective should be to protect your wife." Wycliff's serious stare sent a chill down Benedict's spine. "The attacks will come from every quarter. People will take pleasure in giving her the cut direct. She will quickly come to learn what it was like to walk in your shoes before you found an inner strength."

Benedict stood and tugged the cuffs of his coat. "She may look like she has a backbone of steel, but inside she is as fragile as the woman who rejected me five years ago—ill-prepared for what is to come. She has lived with a misguided notion of what is important and suffered in the process."

Wycliff came to his feet and crossed the room. He gripped Benedict's shoulder. "Perhaps there is hope for you both yet. You defend her with the same burning passion you do when you pretend to despise her."

Oh, when it came to despising Cassandra Mills, he was an expert at pretending. "I want to despise her to the depths of my core. I want to punish her, make her pay. And I want to make love to her, care for her always." God, he was a bloody mess of contradictions.

Wycliff smiled. "The road to fulfilment often involves a perilous journey. Somehow you will reach your destination."

On his return to Jermyn Street, Benedict discovered his wife had commanded use of the drawing room to meet with their housekeeper, Mrs Rampling. He bathed, changed his clothes and retired to his study to examine the letter. A futile exercise in finding a clue to the sender's identity.

Numerous times during the day he crossed paths with Cassandra. They passed pleasantries, spoke about the fact she had brought dinner forward by two hours, a compromise as he was used to eating late. She looked happy, carefree, as if the tragic events of the last few days had never occurred. It was an act, another mask to hide behind because neither knew how to behave, how to be themselves.

They dined at seven, and he was surprised to find a bill of fare enough for a party of six. The menu, more lavish than he preferred with dishes of quail and Parisienne tarts, reminded him of the earl's elitism. His thoughts spiralled into maudlin memories, and before he knew it, the footmen were clearing away the covers and serving them drinks in the drawing room.

They settled into chairs in front of the fire. She took sherry as her digestif. He took port. It was all very structured. Civil. Had they married five years ago, he imagined they would have locked the door, tore off their clothes and made love while the heat from the fire's flames danced over their bare skin. Now, the emptiness inside seemed worse when in her company than when apart.

As they sat in silence, staring into the hearth, he tried to think of something to say. The only thing they had in common was their need to find the brute who'd ruined her life.

"Perhaps we should discuss your attendance at Lord Craven's ball if you feel able."

She jumped upon hearing his voice. "Yes, I've spent the entire day trying to piece together the fragments of that night."

"I presume your father was your chaperone."

"He insisted on accompanying me to every ball and rout."

She looked to her lap as she spoke. "The earl controls everyone and everything, you know that."

"Was Lord Murray there?" Did she slink away to a quiet alcove to share an illicit kiss with her betrothed? Had she crept out into the garden, embraced the lord beneath the moonlight as she had done many times with him?

"Yes."

"Did you dance with Murray?"

"Three times."

"Anything more than dance?" He tried to make it sound like a perfectly reasonable question, yet jealousy imbued his tone. When her shocked eyes met his, he said, "It is important we're honest with each other."

"Does that mean you will afford me the same courtesy?"

"I'm not a hypocrite, Cassandra." Why did he get the impression she relished the prospect of asking personal questions? "You can ask me anything, and I will give you an honest answer."

She swallowed a sip of sherry. "We did nothing of an amorous nature. Timothy believes in the sanctity of marriage and wanted to wait."

Benedict gave a mocking snort. "So he never tried to ravish you? Not a kiss, not an attempt to slip his hand under your skirts and stroke your bare thigh?"

Embarrassment stained her cheeks. "He kissed me when he proposed, but he never touched me the way you used to."

The sound of her sweet sigh when he'd stolen under her skirts and brushed his fingers over her sex would be forever etched in his memory. Desire ignited, desire for the woman he remembered, the woman who hadn't crushed his hopes and dreams.

"While we're on the subject of intimate relations," she said, and he knew what was coming, "have you ever felt affection for the women you've bedded?"

The comment hit him like the splash of ice-cold water,

cooling his heated blood. And he cursed himself for saying he would speak the truth. "Years ago, I vowed only to make love to you, and I have kept my promise. You will think this crude, but you asked for honesty, and so don't be shocked when I tell you that I've cared nothing for the women I've fucked."

Her mouth dropped open, and she snapped it shut. It took her a moment to regain her composure. "Having been certified a virgin by Dr Hadley, I wouldn't know the difference."

Did she have to remind him of the medical man's unnecessary probing? "Trust me, you would know. One carries no emotional connection. The other—" His gaze drifted down the elegant column of her throat, over the swell of milky-white flesh evident above the neckline of her gown. The urge to claim her came upon him. "I imagine the emotional explosion makes the physical pleasure more satisfying."

She stared at him, the fire's amber flames dancing wildly in her eyes. Her lips parted, and for a few seconds he thought of pressing his mouth to hers. Would she taste as sweet as he remembered?

Undoubtedly.

"We should return to the subject of Lord Craven's ball." Benedict shook himself out of his fantasy. "Had you received any threats prior to the event? Is there anyone who could claim to have a grievance against you?"

"No one." She sat there, a perfect picture of innocence. "You might think me a spoilt shrew, but you're the only person with whom I have ever shared cross words."

Benedict snorted. "Perhaps I should be flattered that I raise your passions to such an alarming degree."

"You always stir a reaction in me." She kept her gaze trained on him as she sipped her sherry.

Now his mind turned sinful, and he had to think of another question to distract from the knowledge he could bed his wife whenever he pleased. "So, I'm the only person with a reason to bear a grievance," he mused. "What about Lady Murray? Did she want you to marry her son?"

Cassandra shrugged. "I'm the daughter of an earl, why wouldn't she want to forge an alliance?"

"Because your father has more enemies than I have cravats. Do you know of any disagreement between them?"

"No. They have always been perfectly civil in each other's company."

"And you never doubted Lord Murray's love for you?"

"Not until he scurried from my father's study faster than a rat does a sinking ship."

Benedict laughed. "Forgive me. I do not mean to make light of a distressing situation. It's just I find the image of Murray scampering away somewhat amusing."

It surprised him when Cassandra laughed, too. "You should have seen the look of relief on his face when I freed him from his obligation."

The comment gave him pause.

"You freed Murray?" Benedict sat forward. "But I thought he refused to marry you after hearing of the scandal."

Cassandra relayed the conversation she'd had with the weak-willed lord. "And so, even if he had insisted on keeping his oath, I could not marry a man who would rather drink port and talk politics than comfort his betrothed."

Hmm. Perhaps Cassandra was stronger than he thought.

"Being the focus of a scandal proved quite liberating," she continued. "When one has lost everything, one finds an inner resolve." Her smile faded. "I suppose I will need that when I have to face the gossiping hordes."

The need to protect her burned in his chest. "I've come to learn that it's the meaning we attach to words that causes upset." She would need an education in how to respond to negative comments if she was to survive the vile taunts. "What is a word but a series of muscle movements made in the throat and mouth?"

She seemed to ponder his words. When she met his gaze, water welled in her eyes. "It must have been difficult for you, hearing all the terrible things people said. I said some awful things to you, too, things that make me ashamed."

"I retaliated with equal vehemence."

"When one is consumed with unhappiness, it's easier to cast the blame elsewhere. For years, I have been so angry with you, angry because of your illegitimacy." She dashed a tear from her eye. "These last few days I have never been more grateful for it."

He didn't want to examine the sentiment beneath her observations. Not yet. They had a villain to catch, a devil to snare, and he needed a clear mind if he was to help her carve a new place in society.

"When one faces a battle, it is better to have an ally skilled in combat." He raised his glass in salute before downing the rest of his port. "Tomorrow we should venture into town, meet our adversaries head-on, make a frontal attack."

"You mean we should go out together?"

"Do you think I would let you face them alone?"

Her lips curled into a smile, the first genuine smile he had seen in days. "I should like that. Very much."

He let her wallow in a moment of happiness. Tomorrow they would engage in several skirmishes. They could continue their conversation about the ball while parading through enemy territory. It would occupy her mind, help to detract from the wicked whispers and sly stares.

"Then we should retire early. As well as a shopping trip, we have a rather important gathering to attend tomorrow night."

"A gathering?" She blinked back her surprise. "At Mr Wycliff's house?"

"At the den of the debauched on Theobolds Road. Tomorrow, we will attend a demimonde soirée."

And he would confront Mrs Crandall with his suspicions.

CHAPTER SEVEN

"Perhaps you should go to Theobolds Road alone tonight." Cassandra tightened the silk ribbons of her poke bonnet as she stood in the hall, ready for her outing with Benedict. "You don't need me there when you speak to Mrs Crandall."

During breakfast, Benedict had told her about Mrs Crandall's obsession, about the woman's desperate need to bed him, and she'd sat there, nibbling her toast, surprised to find she had something in common with the queen of the demimonde.

"I want you there." Benedict brushed the lapels of his coat and straightened his black top hat. "Besides, being amongst the demimonde gives one the confidence to deal with the upper echelons." The corners of his mouth curled into a sinful grin. "Trust me. It will be an enlightening experience."

When he smiled like that, how could she refuse?

"I have nothing suitable to wear. It will take days for Madame de La Tour to design a gown daring enough to blend in with those ladies who seek pleasure on the fringes."

Benedict's smile faded at the mention of the famed modiste. "You may have to find another dressmaker." It seemed to pain him to say so.

"Don't be ridiculous. Madame de La Tour has made my gowns since my come-out ball." They were on such friendly terms theirs was more than a business relationship. "She knows what styles suit me."

"Very well. But remember reputation matters just as much to those in trade." He offered his arm. "We'll walk to Piccadilly and up to New Bond Street."

Cassandra slipped her arm through his and clung to the bulging bicep. "And on the way, you must give me an idea of how disgraced women dress."

Benedict led her out onto Jermyn Street. He stopped and drew her round to face him, tucked a strand of hair back into her bonnet and said, "Hold your head high. Never show them their vile words or smug grins hurt you. Do you understand?"

Cassandra swallowed past the lump in her throat. "I understand."

It was a pleasant morning. The crisp air proved refreshing as opposed to leaving one shivering to the soles of their boots. The sun shone brightly, which meant many people would venture out for a leisurely stroll. Ice-cold fear surrounded her heart as she anticipated every frightful encounter. But she didn't have time to dwell on her anxiety as Benedict asked more probing questions about Lord Craven's ball.

"So, we've established you danced with Lord Murray. Did you dance with anyone else?"

"A few gentlemen. Lord Parker. Mr Goddard, and my father forced me to dance with Mr Finch. I was to enquire after his mother's health and try to discover the reason for her dislike of Lady Murray."

Benedict cast her a sidelong glance as they headed towards Piccadilly. "And did Mr Finch tell you anything interesting?"

"Nothing." She often lied to her father rather than embarrass herself by probing into people's personal affairs. "Mr Finch is a buffoon, but I decided against doing my father's bidding and told him Mr Finch knew nothing."

Her heart shot to her throat when they stepped out onto the bustling street of Piccadilly to join the crowd of people going about their daily business. Perhaps it was her imagination, but numerous gentlemen craned their necks to stare. Two ladies giggled, hugged arms and took to whispering as they passed. One couple darted out of her way as if she were a drunken beggar out to accost them for a penny.

Every muscle in her body grew tense as the urge to run and hide took hold. "I'm not sure I can do this, not today." No one had ever looked at her with such disdain and disrespect.

"Courage is a state of mind." Benedict did not seem the least bit affected by the contemptuous glares. "Imagine they've left home this morning and forgotten to dress. Imagine their smug grins fading when they glance in a shop window and see their bare behinds."

Cassandra couldn't help but laugh. "You certainly know what to say to brighten my mood." He always knew what to say to make her happy.

"It works. Watch." They strolled towards Lady Johnson and her less than adorable daughter. The matron recognised them instantly and so stuck her nose in the air and scowled. "Good Lord," Benedict whispered, "those poor people have forgotten to wear clothes."

A snigger burst from Cassandra's lips as she imagined the matron's breasts hanging so low they touched her knees. She stared at the women with a look of shock, contempt and pity. Lady Johnson's ugly expression faded to one of curiosity, then fear, and she gripped her daughter's arm and scurried away without uttering a word.

"Heavens, I feel oddly liberated."

"They won't all be that easy," Benedict warned, "but it's a start."

As always, he was right. Numerous people wore the same look of confusion and mortification when faced with Cassandra's scrutiny. But then the whispers reached her ears. The spiteful comments meant to put paid to her confident demeanour.

"Lord Murray had a lucky escape" was one remark thrown her way.

"A man in government cannot have a hussy for a wife" was another.

"Trollop."

Benedict tried to bolster her defences, but every nasty word hit like a barbed arrow aimed to cause lethal damage. Matters grew progressively worse when they reached New Bond Street and she saw Lord Murray commanding the reins of his racing curricle, looking as pleased with his new equipage as he was the elegant lady seated at his side.

Shame burned Cassandra's cheeks when she met the lord's curious gaze.

"Fine pair of Cleveland Bays, Murray," Benedict called to the lord as they passed. "Weak men always choose spirited horses."

Panic set her body trembling. She gripped Benedict's arm and forced him to continue walking. "Lord Murray has a reputation to uphold. Do you want an invitation to a dawn appointment?"

Benedict gave a mocking snort. "Murray is a coward. I could put him on his arse with my eyes closed. I find his manner unacceptable under the circumstances and would frighten him to within an inch of his life for his indiscretion."

Benedict had a point.

"You'd think he would wait a few days before inviting Miss Pendleton to ride out with him. Could he not at least pretend to be heartbroken?"

"Seeing him openly courting the lady gives him a motive for wanting to break your betrothal." Anger infused Benedict's tone, and he muttered a curse. "If I discover he's responsible, I shall be the one issuing an invitation to meet on the common."

"Because he has ruined your life?"

"No, because he has ruined yours."

A warm, comforting feeling settled in her chest. A lady need fear nothing with Benedict Cavanagh as her husband.

She attempted to analyse why it hurt to see Lord Murray impressing Miss Pendleton with his expert driving. It had nothing to do with mourning a lost love—and she certainly knew how it felt to have her heart wrenched from her chest. While she had held Murray in high esteem, she never felt as though she might die without his touch. No. It had more to do with the fact she had been used and discarded by people she trusted.

"Lord Murray hasn't ruined my life, Benedict. He's made me evaluate what is important."

She pulled Benedict to the window of Craddock and Haines bookshop. Not to look at the autumnal palette of leather-bound books, but to study their reflection in the glass. They looked like any other respectable couple, yet their relationship had been marred by people eager to interfere.

"Hellfire, they have a copy of *Vathek*." Benedict took her hand and pulled her into the bookshop. He left her perusing the volumes on the shelves while he asked to look at the supernatural tale on display.

Keen to avoid other disagreeable members of the *ton*, she headed to the shelves near the back of the shop. Noting a lady dressed in widow's weeds peering curiously at the books, Cassandra decided to make a hasty retreat. But the woman swung around, and their gazes locked.

"Sybil?"

Sybil tapped her finger frantically to her lips and then beckoned Cassandra forward.

"Why are you hiding back here?" Cassandra whispered.

Sybil pointed to the thin gap between the row of books, a gap that afforded a view of a gentleman with raven black hair devouring the mouth of an elegant lady in the next aisle.

Cassandra shrugged in confusion. "Who are they?" With the amorous couple locked in a passionate embrace, one could not distinguish any telling features. "And why are you dressed in black? You always wear green."

"It's my disguise." Sybil pressed her finger to her lips again. Carefully, she moved the books to close the gap and stepped back from the shelves. "Do you remember me telling you about Devious Daventry?"

"You mean Lucius Daventry?"

"Yes, but the man is as unscrupulous as the devil and deserves the moniker. I heard that he is holding a private auction to sell the journals and scientific apparatus he bought from my father. As you know, I'm keen to buy them back. When I wrote to him and asked for a seat at the sale, he refused."

Sybil was obsessed with securing the return of her father's possessions. It had to do with a cryptic clue for something or other, but it was often difficult to follow the erratic train of Sybil's thoughts.

"And so you are stalking the gentleman in the hope of learning the whereabouts of this secret location?"

"Precisely. Mr Daventry is not the only one who possesses a cunning mind."

"You should have a care. Of all the illegitimate sons of the aristocracy, Mr Daventry is considered the most dangerous."

"Dangerous when it comes to seducing women into bed, but I am hardly his type." Sybil glanced over Cassandra's shoulder and almost jumped out of her skin. "Wait. My quarry is on the move. Indeed, Satan's spawn has stopped to speak to your husband. Blessed saints! They're laughing like old friends. Perhaps Mr Cavanagh knows about the auction." Sybil grabbed Cassandra's hands. "Oh, would you speak to your husband and see if he knows anything about the sale? Now, I must dash. I shall come and visit you in Jermyn Street in the next few days."

Sybil tucked a strand of hair into her black bonnet and darted past. She lingered in the doorway, peering around the jamb before hurrying out onto New Bond Street.

Cassandra returned to Benedict, feeling as if she had just survived a whirlwind. "Did you make a purchase?"

"No, I wanted to see if anyone had written on the blank page. They hadn't." When Cassandra frowned, he added, "Trent met his wife, Verity, when they were solving a mystery involving the book. It's a long story. I shall relay the tale tonight after dinner."

"I didn't know you were acquainted with Mr Daventry." She couldn't lie to her husband and so told him about her odd conversation with Sybil. "Has he mentioned an auction?"

"Not to me, but I can make enquiries." He took her hand and placed it in the crook of his arm. "Are you ready to go home now, or do you need to gaze upon the naked members of the aristocracy some more?"

His amusing comment made her smile. Having him as her greatest supporter made everything seem right with the world. She hadn't felt this close to him since before she told him he was not good enough to marry.

That thought brought a tear to her eye, and she dashed it away. "I would like to visit Madame de La Tour. Perhaps she might have a suggestion as to what I can wear tonight. I think something vibrant, don't you?"

His mood turned suddenly subdued.

"Don't seem so downcast." She drew him further along the street. "I understand if you'd prefer to wait outside. Most gentlemen find the topic of ladies' fripperies tedious."

"Then be thankful I'm a scoundrel who likes ogling scanty undergarments." Though he spoke in jest, she sensed concern for her welfare was the reason he insisted on accompanying her into the modiste's shop.

Cassandra knew visiting the madame was a mistake as soon as she stepped over the threshold. The hum of conversation died. Madame de La Tour's assistants clutched their samples of rich velvets and sumptuous satins and froze. The few customers perusing the madame's wares turned to face the two newcomers hovering near the door.

Benedict clasped Cassandra's elbow and propelled her forward, past the sour-faced matron who mumbled, "Foolish gel."

Madame de La Tour's modiste shop carried the same air of opulence as an aristocrat's ballroom. The heavy scent of perfume irritated the nostrils. Light shone through the large windows, bouncing off the full-length mirrors and the teardrop crystals of the chandelier. One almost expected to find a wallflower hiding behind a large potted fern—a bluestocking seated on the burgundy chaise.

The two ladies at the counter said something to Valerine, the madame's assistant, and then left the shop in feverish haste.

With Benedict by her side, Cassandra stepped closer to the counter. "Good day, Valerine. I don't have an appointment but would like to see your madame for a moment."

The young woman responded with a curt nod and disappeared into the private fitting room. A few moments later, Madame de La Tour appeared. She walked towards them with the deportment of a duchess. Her thin face and pointed chin were more in keeping with a stern governess than a modiste.

Still, the madame smiled as she greeted them. "My lady."

"It is Mrs Cavanagh now. I recently married."

"*Oui, bien sûr*. People, they are saying you married Lord Tregarth's son."

No doubt news of their nuptials had spread quicker than a fire in a hay barn. Sharing the latest snippets of gossip eased the boredom of having a dress fitting.

"Indeed, which is why I must make an appointment to discuss a new wardrobe." Cassandra leaned closer, intending to ask how one dressed to appear more alluring, as she had nothing remotely suitable for a demimonde soirée. But the madame's disinterested look gave her pause.

"I'm afraid I 'ave no appointments available." The woman swallowed deeply, a clear sign she was lying.

"No appointments this week?" Cassandra attempted to clarify. A mix of anger and mortification surfaced. "Or no appointments you are willing to grant me."

The modiste shuffled uncomfortably. "You must understand, I dress the debutantes from the wealthiest families," she said in a thick French burr. "The mere 'int of a scandal and the aristocracy they take their custom elsewhere."

"I am still the daughter of an earl. Does that count for nothing?"

"Madame, I must think of my reputation."

"Well, at least we understand one another."

She half expected Benedict to chastise the woman for her hypocrisy, but he simply said, "Thank you, madame, for your tact and honesty. Good day." And then he clasped Cassandra's elbow and guided her out onto New Bond Street.

The hustle and bustle of the busy street proved suffocating. There were so many people. People staring. People pointing. People thinking vile thoughts.

"Take me home, Benedict. I've had enough for today." The thought of walking back to Jermyn Street through the disapproving crowds filled her with dread.

"Certainly. I instructed Foston to follow in the carriage. He is waiting a little further along the road. After a busy hour spent shopping, I thought you might prefer to drive home than suffer the long walk."

The need to throw her arms around Benedict's neck and kiss him took hold. "I should have listened to you. You're the intelligent one. I'm the fool who makes countless mistakes."

"You've lived in a world where everyone wears masks. I'm one of the lucky few who have seen what really lies behind their fake smiles and forced manners." Benedict motioned to Foston, who sat atop the carriage parked outside the milliner's shop, and she resisted the urge to grip her husband's hand and race towards the vehicle. "Blame those with the power to change society's attitude, not those whose livelihoods depend upon recommendations."

Admiration warmed her chest. Wisdom and strength radiated from every aspect of his being. After hearing the salacious rumours, she expected to find him much changed. Arrogant. Bitter. Cynical. But he bore the same air of calm confidence, coupled with a supreme understanding of life.

"I cannot be angry at the modiste," she said as Benedict assisted her into the carriage and muttered an instruction to his coachman. "She declined my custom to protect her reputation. I declined the prospect of marrying you to save mine. I am more of a hypocrite than she could ever be."

Her father had been so persuasive. Benedict had been so hurt. She was the villain. The undutiful daughter. The disloyal love. She wore the names like labels sewn to her chest. Now she could add more to the list. Immoral harlot. Disgraced fool.

Benedict dropped into the seat opposite as the carriage lurched forward. He remained silent—lost in thoughtful contemplation. Undoubtedly her comment about not marrying him to save her reputation had caused his sudden change in mood.

"My father spent years convincing me you weren't good enough," she said. The constant barrage had worn her down, weakened her already feeble resolve. "If these last few days have taught me anything, it's that I am the one who is inferior."

He raised his head and their gazes collided. She saw her own pain reflected back, but how did one even begin to repair the damage?

"Tell me something nice, something you remember about me before my father sought to separate us for good." Her voice cracked, and her vision became blurry. Crying did little to ease the pain of regret. "Something that might restore my self-worth."

His gaze softened, and a slow, sensual smile formed. The smile that wrung knots in her stomach and made her giddy. "You used to believe that majestic things grew from small beginnings." He crossed the carriage to sit beside her. "You used to believe in the power of love. I felt the strength of your conviction every time we kissed."

She swallowed deeply as the memory of his hot mouth on hers sent her pulse racing. Oh, she would give anything to go back in time, to feel the depth of his love again. "And now I am dead inside."

"You're not dead inside, Cassandra." He cupped her cheek, and it took immense effort not to grab his hand and hug it to her breast. "You're lost and need to find yourself again."

He made her problems sound simple to resolve.

"But where do I start?" She didn't belong anywhere. The demimonde would consider her too prim to join their fold. Society had closed its doors and barred the hatches.

"You start with an acorn. You nurture it and watch it grow."

"Then I need to go back to the younger woman, the woman I've not known for five years." The woman who had kissed him under the willow tree before she ripped out her heart and handed it to her father to discard with his other useless trophies. "Would you do something for me?" It was selfish to ask. He had already done so much.

His frown revealed a certain hesitance, but he said, "I'm your husband. It's my duty to make you happy."

She gulped past her nerves. "Help me to remember. Kiss me like you used to all those years ago, before all the hatred and bitterness. Help me build a solid foundation, a place to start."

A brief silence ensued, broken only by the strained sound of his breathing. "You ask for something I cannot give."

Rejection caused a searing pain in her heart. "I understand. You cannot forget all the terrible things I've said and done." And who could blame him?

"It's not that," he said, shuffling closer. "You ask for the tender, loving kiss of a young man. All I can promise is the lustful kiss of a scoundrel."

The sudden pulsing between her thighs urged her to take

whatever he had to give. “You said I should start with small beginnings. I haven’t the first notion what it’s like to be kissed by a lustful scoundrel.”

Benedict moistened his lips. “Then let me show you.”

CHAPTER EIGHT

Numerous times during their outing to town, Benedict had imagined drawing Cassandra into an embrace and kissing away her doubts and fears. Many times during his late-night visit to Hyde Park, he'd thought of racing home to claim his bride. Pride prevented him from acting. When a man had suffered the worst kind of rejection, he approached all romantic liaisons with an air of caution.

But his wife had asked for a kiss. Not a chaste peck, but the sinful kiss of a scoundrel, and he was happy to oblige. He knew how to seduce a woman without complicated entanglements and heightened emotions. Perhaps he'd been wrong in the belief that a man had to make love to his wife. Perhaps lust was a perfect foundation for marriage.

He took hold of Cassandra's chin, angled his head and pressed his mouth to hers. Instantly, he was hit with the same violent jolt of awareness he experienced whenever they touched. The muscles in his stomach clenched. His body hardened. His blood burned in his veins. He closed his eyes and inhaled the sweet scent of the woman who always sent his world spinning on its axis.

Damnation!

His control was slipping before he'd barely begun. That's what happened when a man focused his mind on the urges of his body, not the fanciful musings of his heart.

"Straddle me," he demanded, pretending this was just another opportunity to fornicate with a courtesan in the privacy of one's carriage. He leant forward and yanked down the blinds. "Sit astride me, Cassandra."

She seemed confused and fumbled about trying to follow his command without lifting her skirts.

Benedict clutched her hem and gathered her skirts up past her knees. The sight of her white stockings sent blood rushing to his cock. Lust vibrated through his veins as his wife parted her legs and came to sit on top of him.

God, he was harder than he'd ever been in his life.

He cupped her nape and dragged her mouth to his. With the tip of his tongue, he coaxed her lips apart and devoured her in a wild and wicked kiss that left him hungry. Ravenous. He plunged into her mouth with the same fervent passion he would her body. Their tongues tangled, mated, fucked, every wet caress tugging at his insides as his ballocks grew tight and heavy. Soon, their moans and breathless pants rent the air.

Struggling to control his raging desire, he continued to feast while unfastening her jacket. Once undone, he yanked the material apart to reveal the soft swell of milky-white flesh. Perfect. How he longed to free her breasts and lavish her nipples with attention. How he longed to open her legs and push deep inside her tight body. To ride her so damn hard he would forget her past betrayal.

But he sensed the carriage slowing and so tore his mouth from hers, leaving her panting. Wanting. Needing him.

"Touch me like you used to," she breathed, writhing against his erection. "My body is aching to feel you again."

Bloody hell!

The minx was set to make him spill in his breeches.

But the carriage rocked and rolled to a halt, and along with it came the depressing sense they had reached their destination.

"If you're willing, we might continue our exploration in the carriage this evening." Now he had tasted her again he doubted he had the will to keep his hands to himself.

Cassandra struggled to catch her breath. The haze of desire in her blue eyes dazzled him. Then her lips curled into a smile, and she looked at him in the sensual way she used to long before they were enemies.

"I would be willing to sample more lustful kisses. Indeed, I have never felt so alive."

How would she feel when he was thrusting inside her? When her body soared on the dizzying heights of her release? Would she marvel at the skill of his tongue? Would she curse herself for rejecting him?

Benedict couldn't resist stroking her breasts as he set about fastening her jacket. "Would you mind moving to the opposite seat," he said once he'd finished the task. "I cannot enter Mrs Seymour's home with an erection straining against my breeches." He forced an image of Mrs Crandall into his mind, which soon dampened his ardour.

"Mrs Seymour? You mean we've not gone directly home?"

"No." And he was thankful for his foresight. He needed time to adjust, time to gauge the best course of action now he'd ignited his wife's passions. "You need a suitable gown for this evening, and Valerie will know what to do."

"Valerie?" Jealousy and suspicion clung to that one word. "Is she a lady you know from the demimonde?"

"Valerie is my father's mistress," he said, unable to suppress a grin, "and a friend."

"Oh! So your father has given up trying to sire an heir?"

Tregarth had been widowed three times, lost his only legitimate son and heir in childbirth. The Earl of Worthen was marred by a similar misfortune.

"Having a mistress would not stop my father marrying. But

he no longer has an interest in securing his bloodline. The estate will pass to a cousin, and I shall inherit everything unentailed. He regards me as some sort of miracle."

"Your father loves you. His affection shines in his eyes whenever you're in the same room."

"His love helped me through the most difficult time of my life." Benedict had no memory of his mother, but his father had been full of compassion and wisdom when Cassandra refused his suit. "Consequently, I cannot condemn him for his rakish behaviour."

"Does he love Mrs Seymour?"

Benedict shrugged. "Who can say? I'm not sure he's capable of loving a woman."

"Everyone is capable of romantic love," she said with some amusement, but then her smile faded. "Except for my father. He's cold when it comes to anything other than advancing his position."

Before the mood turned depressing, Benedict shuffled to the edge of the seat and straightened his coat. He leaned forward to brush a crease from her skirt and Cassandra's excited gasp confirmed she welcomed his advances.

"Come, let me introduce you to Valerie. She'll find you something disgraceful to wear to a demimonde soirée."

Benedict waited for an hour in Valerie's drawing room while the lady played modiste to his wife. When the women returned, they took to whispering and casting knowing smirks in his direction. They explained that the maid needed to make alterations to the gown, and it would be best if Cassandra remained in Valerie's care until Benedict called to take her to Mrs Crandall's depraved den.

An uncomfortable prickle rippled across his shoulders at the thought of trusting someone else with his wife's safety. But then

Tregarth arrived, and so Benedict kept his father company while the ladies ventured upstairs.

Hours passed, leaving him barely enough time to head back to Jermyn Street to bathe and change into suitable attire.

Upon his return, Valerie instructed Benedict to wait in the hall while she went upstairs to call Cassandra. His wife appeared soon after, dressed in a sumptuous red velvet gown trimmed with gold brocade.

Good Lord!

He held his breath as he drank in the delightful sight.

The sleeves skimmed her shoulders, accentuating the elegant column of her throat. The scandalously low neckline drew the eye to the soft swell of her breasts. And yet that wasn't what made him want to take her in his arms and ravish her senseless. No. It was the bright glint of happiness in her eyes that made him want her. It was the confident way she descended the stairs and the unspoken words that passed between them.

He stared at her for the longest time, trying to contain the roiling emotions in his chest. "You look divine," he whispered when she reached the bottom step. He swallowed past the lump in his throat as he noted the teasing curl draped over her shoulder. "Alluring. Elegant."

"Valerie is as talented as Madame de La Tour when it comes to how a woman should dress."

He could not argue.

"Doesn't she look wonderful?" Valerie's voice captured Benedict's attention.

"She always looks wonderful." He found Cassandra attractive with bird nest hair and wearing a dirty chemise. "But yes, you have exceeded yourself, Valerie."

"The advantage of red is it suits most women," Valerie said.

Indeed, Valerie was twenty years Cassandra's senior with ebony hair streaked grey at the temples. Tregarth preferred mature women to the young widows gracing the ballrooms.

"You wore red the first night we were introduced." Tregarth

appeared at the drawing room door, cradling a glass of brandy. He leant against the jamb, looked relaxed in just his shirt sleeves.

Valerie smiled. "You remember."

"I shall never forget."

Benedict cleared his throat. "Well, we have taken enough of your time and shall leave you to enjoy the rest of your evening. We have a soirée to attend."

Tregarth straightened and stepped out into the hall. "I shall be here all night should you need me."

After thanking Valerie for her assistance, Benedict escorted Cassandra to their carriage. They had not spoken privately since their heated kiss hours earlier. Being in the confined space brought the memories flooding back.

"You should prepare yourself for what you might encounter this evening," he said. Despite all that had occurred, she was still an innocent at heart. "The rogues who attend Mrs Crandall's events have no conscience. Their morals are rather lax."

She shuffled nervously for the umpteenth time. "You mean they might say lewd things?"

"I mean don't be surprised if you see people partaking in illicit acts."

"Illicit acts?" Her eyes widened, and then recognition dawned. "Oh! I see."

"You're married to a rogue, so there's nothing to fear." That wasn't entirely true. Mrs Crandall could be devious, ruthless when provoked. "Though I must insist you remain by my side for the entire evening."

She snorted. "I have no intention of letting go of your arm."

A vivid image of reckless fornicators brought a smile to his lips. "Witnessing lustful displays often arouse one's own desires."

She raised her chin as a blush stained her cheeks. "I'm sure I shall find it all rather distasteful."

"I'm sure you will."

The carriage rumbled to a halt outside Mrs Crandall's abode on Theobolds Road. Benedict opened the carriage door and vaulted to the pavement. Cassandra reached out for his assistance, but he settled his hands on her trim waist and lowered her slowly down to the ground.

The need to kiss her came upon him again.

She clutched his upper arms as he drew her close to his chest. "Is embracing in the street part of my initiation?"

The rogue in him surfaced. "No, consider this a means to stimulate the appetite." He captured her mouth in a kiss as sinful as it was quick.

"Goodness." She blinked rapidly and then a chuckle escaped her. "Perhaps we should attend Mrs Crandall's gatherings every evening."

"Perhaps we should arrange a gathering of our own."

She screwed up her nose. "And invite people to use our home as a brothel?"

"Who said we need to invite anyone else?"

Excitement danced in her eyes. Just as it had done all those years ago when she'd crept out of her father's country house after dark to meet him secretly in the shadows. He might have kissed her again, but another carriage turned into the street, and so he knocked on Mrs Crandall's door with a unique series of raps known only to those selected to attend.

Woods, Mrs Crandall's majordomo, opened the door. His eyes widened upon seeing Benedict, widening still as his lecherous gaze lingered on the bountiful expanse of Cassandra's breasts. "Mr Cavanagh. Speak to me before you leave." Woods glanced back over his shoulder before whispering, "I've more information to sell should you be willing to pay."

Curiosity burned, but Benedict nodded and guided his wife over the threshold into the underworld haven for sinners.

As always, thick tobacco smoke hung in the air like a sinister mist, a hazy curtain between good and evil, right and wrong. The musky scent of lust teased the senses, as did the moans of those couples frolicking in the dim hallway.

Cassandra clutched his arm. The exotic aroma of her perfume had men tearing their mouths away from their lovers like hungry wolves sniffing out a foreign scent. They nodded respectfully to him, though that didn't stop them stripping Cassandra naked beneath hooded eyes. Indeed, the men's penetrating stares followed them to the drawing room as did the whispered echoes of her name.

"Heavens." She sucked in a sharp breath as she scanned those lounging half-dressed on the sofas. What they had enjoyed in the privacy of their carriage was displayed here for all to see. "And I thought you were exaggerating, preparing me for the worst."

"I always speak the truth."

A guttural groan and a woman's rapid pants emanated from behind the thick red curtains. "See. Some people still require privacy."

Benedict snorted. "And yet everyone will hear the moment she climaxes."

From the bemused look on Cassandra's face, it was evident she knew nothing of the pleasures a woman experienced in the bedchamber.

"Later, when we're alone, I shall explain exactly what I mean," he said, anticipating the moment Cassandra shuddered beneath him while finding her release. "Marriage to me will be an education in more ways than one."

"In all honesty, I find I'm an eager student."

Thoughts of fleeing this iniquitous place surfaced, but he was forced to remember why they had come. "First, we must focus on the task at hand," he said, snatching two glasses of champagne from the console table and giving one to his wife.

"Yes, to discover if Mrs Crandall is the one responsible for my ruination." Cassandra craned her neck. "Can you see her?"

Benedict did not need to look far. As soon as he scanned the room, he locked gazes with the red-haired vixen. Her stone-like expression never faltered, even when she made her apologies to the dissolute son of Lord Aiken and strode across the room to greet them.

"Mrs Cavanagh, it's a pleasure to make your acquaintance." Resentment festered behind Mrs Crandall's fake smile, a smile that slipped from her face the moment her attention shifted to him. "Benedict. You're full of surprises. You swore never to marry."

Mrs Crandall was a fountain of knowledge when it came to gossip and scandal, so there was little point skirting around the truth. "What else can two people do when caught in a compromising position? A position forced upon them by someone out for revenge."

"Revenge?" The madam slapped her hand to her chest and feigned shock. "I'm sure no one has a gripe with you, Benedict." She glanced at Cassandra. "No doubt your father picked the wrong enemy in his bid to control the world."

"That would be the obvious conclusion," Cassandra replied. "Or perhaps the perpetrator simply wished to hurt me."

Benedict sipped his champagne and studied the madam as she said in a mocking tone, "Hurt you? You're married to Benedict Cavanagh. Whoever conspired to bring this about must care for you a great deal. A woman would sell her soul to spend a night in his bed."

"Or Cassandra is right," he said, quick to move away from the madam's passions. "She was the intended target and the person responsible never dreamed I would marry a woman I despised."

Mrs Crandall laughed. "One might drive oneself insane in their search for the answer. Is it not better to accept your fate? Marriage needn't stop either of you from satisfying your own need for pleasure." The woman's sensual gaze trailed a line from his mouth down to his groin. "And what better punishment for an earl obsessed with his bloodline than to deny him a grandchild."

Mrs Crandall was a fool if she thought he would forgo the pleasure of being a father just to spite Worthen. Their children would be legitimate. Would never have to suffer as he had done. But then the thought that the earl would always see their offspring as inferior caused a sudden surge of anger.

"I have kept my opinions to myself for far too long," he said, his voice as stern as he intended. "So I ask you, did you play a part in what happened to my wife?"

Mrs Crandall jerked as if reeling from a slap. "Me? Good Lord. I would never ruin an innocent to get what I want. How the devil do you think I ended up here? Indeed, had I known you would be forced to marry, I may have intervened. I might have saved her reputation. McCreath is loyal to your father. Drummond would do anything to advance his career. Had you both come to me, freedom might have been yours."

Freedom?

He'd come to believe that *freedom* was just another word for *loneliness*.

"And what of Purcell?" Benedict countered. "He met privately with you. More than once. Do you deny it?"

The madam narrowed her gaze. "Who told you that?"

"You're not the only one who trades secrets."

Mrs Crandall arched a coy brow. "Then what do you have to trade?" She moistened her rouged lips. "If you want to learn a secret, you must have something to offer in return. I'm sure your wife won't mind if we slip away for a time. She seems as eager as you to learn the truth."

"Benedict does have something to offer," Cassandra interjected. "He has something precious. Something priceless."

"Priceless, indeed. Few men have his skill in the bedchamber."

"I am not referring to his prowess."

"What then?"

"His respect."

Mrs Crandall appeared bemused.

"Trust me," Cassandra continued with confidence. "When a man you care about despises you, it's like a disease eating away at your heart. I would rather have Benedict's respect. I would rather have his gratitude than his disdain." When the corners of Mrs Crandall's lips curled into a smile, Cassandra added, "I imagine there are many men here who can satisfy your physical needs. Men with equal skill."

Mrs Crandall glanced at the two men watching her from the opposite side of the room before turning back to Cassandra. "There are some who might prove adequate. The question is, would Benedict's respect ease my craving?"

Benedict captured the madam's hand and pressed a kiss to her bare knuckles. "Speak honestly to me, help me in my endeavour, and you will have my untold gratitude and respect."

The woman's eyes flamed hot. "Has anyone told you, you're an extremely charismatic man? Even with your clothes on." She didn't wait for a reply. "Come. Let me take you both to my private parlour."

They followed Mrs Crandall to a locked room overlooking Theobolds Road. The room where Trent had threatened the majordomo only a few weeks before. She motioned for them to sit on the sofa, locked the door and moved to the seat opposite.

"So you wish to know why Lord Purcell sought a private audience?" she said, relaxing back in the chair.

"Yes. I want to know if he kidnapped and drugged my wife."

After a moment's contemplation, Mrs Crandall sighed. "Purcell knows I buy secrets. I keep them close to my chest, and I use them when needed. Every person in the *ton* has something to hide. Secrets grant a person more power than money or position ever could. Purcell wished to know if I had any information on Lord Worthen."

"Lord Worthen?" Cassandra sat forward. "You know my father's secrets?"

"I know your father bribed a man to ensure he secured a property in Shropshire. When I heard of Purcell's suspicions, I sought the clerk who collected the tenders."

Cassandra snorted. "Lord Purcell is wealthy enough to pay the clerk for information. Why would he need to come to you?"

"Because the clerk cannot be bribed with money. Lord Worthen holds the deeds to the house where the clerk's unmarried sister lived with her child. He threatened to evict them unless the clerk co-operated."

"The clerk would face prosecution if people discovered he acted fraudulently," Benedict said, struggling to shake his disgust for his father-in-law's actions.

"Which is why I offered the clerk's sister alternative accommodation in exchange for information. And Lord Worthen can no longer threaten the clerk as both men are guilty of a crime."

Benedict had to admire Mrs Crandall's cunning. "And did you trade the secret with Purcell?"

"No. It is mine to use should Lord Worthen ever pose a problem. Besides, Purcell had nothing to offer in exchange. However, he did ask if I knew why you despise each other. Apparently, it is common knowledge throughout the *ton*. Then he asked if I had information on Lord Tregarth."

Good God!

Benedict's father would beat Purcell to within an inch of his life if he knew the devious lord was prying into his affairs.

"You cannot have anything on my father," Benedict said with confidence. "Tregarth has always been honest with me."

Mrs Crandall smiled. "Even if I had knowledge of Tregarth's affairs, I would never betray you, Benedict." She paused. "Purcell returned a second time. He said he'd heard I had a particular fondness for you and offered me an opportunity to hurt those who had caused you distress."

"Hell and damnation!" Benedict gritted his teeth and shot to his feet. "The conniving—"

"Then Lord Purcell is responsible for what happened to me."

Cassandra's shoulders slumped, and she breathed a weary sigh. "I'm an easy target for those who seek to punish my father."

"Purcell would seem the most likely candidate." Mrs Crandall rose from the chair. She stepped closer and offered her hand. "For one more show of respect, Benedict, I might share another secret."

He didn't hesitate and bowed over the madam's hand. "Any information that may enlighten us as to the perpetrator's motive will be most welcome."

Mrs Crandall's eyes twinkled. "Lord Murray squandered half his yearly income last month alone. His mother does her best to hide her son's reckless spending, but I'm told the situation is growing rather desperate. Perhaps it is wise to consider his need to marry a lady with a substantial dowry. A lady who has a generous father when it comes to bestowing monetary gifts to his family. And that is not Lord Worthen."

The news did not come as a shock.

The *ton* was a walking monument to hypocrisy.

"Now," Mrs Crandall continued, "unless you're here to frolic and fornicate, I shall ask that you take your leave." She unlocked the door and led them out into the hallway. "Woods, show our guests out, would you?"

Woods plodded slowly to the front door. He lingered, waiting for his mistress to head back to the drawing room so he might sell the information he had alluded to earlier. But like a hawk, Mrs Crandall watched his every move.

"Say good night, Woods." The madam's expression turned hard, unyielding. "And before you return to your duties, I want to see you in my private parlour. It seems we have a little bird in our midst who likes to tweet tales."

CHAPTER NINE

"Do you believe her?" Cassandra took hold of Benedict's arm as they waited on the pavement outside Mrs Crandall's abode. "Do you believe what she said about Lord Murray's excessive spending?" She was skirting around the question she wanted to ask. Had Timothy conspired to ruin her to secure a better financial arrangement?

"You saw Murray's new racing curricle and Cleveland Bays." Benedict gestured to their coachman, who'd parked the carriage at the end of the road. "Murray likes to flaunt his wealth. Those who lean towards ostentatious displays of grandeur often have empty pockets."

"But Lady Murray is a pillar of respectability." The lady professed to have the morals of a saint. Had Cassandra not released Timothy from his obligation, his mother would have found a way to disentangle her son. "I'm surprised she hasn't curbed his spending."

With a huff of frustration, Benedict raised his hand and beckoned Foston again, yet the coachman failed to sit up straight or flick the reins. "The man must have fallen asleep."

"Do you suppose Miss Pendleton's brother offered a dowry

more substantial than mine? I have heard the viscount is keen to be rid of his burden, keen to see his sister wed."

"If Murray needs money, it makes sense to look for an excuse to sever ties with you and search elsewhere." Benedict captured her hand and led her along the street. "Come, we'll be chilled to the bone if we wait for Foston."

"Then, the Murrays have a motive to ruin my reputation. My father would have insisted on some form of recompense had Lord Murray expressed a wish to end our betrothal." She panted for breath as she hurried to keep his fast pace. "And Timothy had ample opportunity to drug my drink at the ball."

How could a man profess love and yet act so cruelly?

"If Murray was seen helping you into a carriage, no one would suspect anything untoward." A curse burst from his lips. "Murray will find himself staring down the barrel of a pistol if he's guilty."

A shiver of trepidation ran from her neck to her navel. While she wanted to punish the person responsible, part of her wanted to forget about the shameful event in Hyde Park and concentrate on mending her relationship with Benedict.

"I suspect Mrs Crandall is in love with you," she said, eager to banish all thoughts of Timothy's betrayal. No one liked being taken for a fool.

In heavens name! she thought, chastising herself. Was she not a dreadful hypocrite? She had betrayed the only person who should have mattered. And for what? To please her father? To make amends for the fact her mother died in childbirth? A lifetime spent loving Benedict would not atone for what she had done.

"Power is the only thing Mrs Crandall craves." Benedict motioned to Foston for the umpteenth time. "The woman is obsessed with dominating men. The fact I refuse her advances only makes her more determined to succeed."

Mrs Crandall wasn't the only woman at the soirée to strip

Benedict naked with hungry eyes. It had taken effort not to lay claim to him. Jealousy still writhed in her chest.

"Benedict, I know I'm not in a position to make demands, but we need to discuss what we expect from this marriage." Knots formed in her stomach. "Mrs Crandall raised a valid point." She inhaled deeply. "I know it is too soon to consider the prospect of children, but—" She cast him a sidelong glance and noted his narrow gaze focused on his coachman. "If you'd rather not speak—"

"Hush a moment," he whispered. "We will discuss our marriage later. For now, I need you to play the doting wife and kiss me." He drew her to an abrupt halt a few feet from the carriage and swung her around to face him. "Kiss me on the cheek. Make this look like another amorous interlude."

She was about to ask why but noted the flash of apprehension in his eyes. Trusting Benedict had never been a problem, and so she ran her hands over his chest and kissed him as he'd asked.

He returned her display of affection by nuzzling her neck and whispering, "Don't be alarmed, but that is not Foston sitting atop the box."

Don't be alarmed!

Every muscle in her body grew rigid.

Panic stole the breath from her lungs.

"While I'm kissing you, look into the carriage and tell me what you see." The feel of Benedict's hot mouth pressed against the sensitive skin below her ear sent her head spinning. "Try to concentrate."

That was easier said than done when her body thrummed with the threat of danger. When she had to shake herself sober from the dizzying effects of desire. Her head lolled to one side as Benedict continued his illicit ministrations. "There are people inside the carriage, though it's difficult to see how many. No one waiting behind the vehicle."

"So, I'll assume there are four men and Foston. That shouldn't be a problem unless they're armed."

"We could run back to Mrs Crandall's house," she muttered before switching roles and sucking on his earlobe.

"Hell, woman, must you be so convincing?" He kissed her once on the mouth. "When the fight starts, run to Mrs Crandall's."

The fight?

But Benedict was outnumbered. The odds were against him. She wanted to grab his lapels and shake sense into his addled brain, but he released his grip on her waist and turned to the man sitting atop the box whose raised collars almost met the brim of his hat.

"Take us home, Foston."

"Aye, sir." The imposter's gravelly voice sounded rougher than Foston's.

"Stand back," Benedict whispered to her before stepping up to the carriage door and wrapping his fingers around the handle.

Everything happened so quickly then.

Benedict wrenched open the door. His guttural growl rent the air as he reached into the carriage, grabbed one man by his coat lapels and dragged him out onto the pavement. The brute hit the ground hard, arms flailing. Benedict's powerful kick to the stomach left the fiend writhing in agony.

A riot started in the carriage. The conveyance rocked wildly back and forth as Foston and two other men exchanged punches.

Benedict took a pugilist's stance as the fake coachman approached wielding a riding crop in one hand and a blade in the other.

"Come on, yer cowardly bastard." The man snarled and swiped the air with the blade. "Let's see what they taught yer in dancin' school."

Benedict snorted as he bounced lightly on his feet and shifted his weight gracefully. "I may be a bastard, but I'm no coward."

Cassandra stood helpless.

Benedict had told her to run to Mrs Crandall, but she didn't know the strange knock that brought the majordomo to the door. Still, she had to do something.

The brute on the pavement reached out to grab Benedict's ankle, and so Cassandra rushed forward and stamped on his hand. When he clutched the hem of her gown, she stamped on his arm repeatedly until he let go and cried, "The bitch has damned near broken my arm."

The rumpus in the carriage tumbled out onto the street. All three men fell out of the carriage door, fists flying as they grappled and wrestled each other to the ground. Foston got to his feet and then delivered a blow that sent one man hurtling into the air. Foston's savage roar saw both his opponents scramble up and break into a run as the coachman chased them into the night.

Cassandra's attention shot to Benedict as his attacker shuffled closer, jabbing the air with his knife. Her husband continued to watch his prey with the keenness of a hawk. With skill and impressive agility, he avoided the vicious thrusts. And then, quicker than a lightning strike, he grabbed the miscreant's wrist and twisted until the man released his grip on the weapon. The blade went skimming across the pavement and under the carriage's chassis.

That didn't stop the devil's violent pursuit. He continued his assault by whipping Benedict across the back with the crop.

"Benedict!" she cried when her husband took a punch to the face that almost knocked him clean off his feet.

Somehow he remained standing. Somehow he continued to fight back. Despite society's efforts to subdue him, Benedict never surrendered. No other man of her acquaintance bore the same strength of heart and mind.

Pride and admiration and the love she'd felt for him long ago brought a feverish excitement to her chest. The desperate longing she'd battled to suppress surfaced. Benedict Cavanagh was a magnificent specimen of a man. Indeed, when he wrenched the crop from the devil's hands and cast the weapon aside, when he hit his opponent so hard the blackguard's nose cracked, she knew he would be victorious.

She was so enthralled by her husband that she almost forgot the rogue's accomplice. The snake clutched his injured arm to his chest and slithered along the ground to grab the discarded crop. But Cassandra picked it up and hit out at the man just as he found the strength to lunge at her.

She fell back, landed so hard she jarred her neck as she tried to stop her head hitting the pavement.

"If it's money you want, I have none," she cried as the snake tried to wrestle the crop from her grasp. She kicked out, but her skirts wrapped around her legs. "Get off me!"

The monster snarled and licked his lips. The jagged scar above his top lip was more prominent now, and his eyes reminded her of a feral beast, black with slivers of gold. Indeed, his incisors looked as sharp as that of any predatory animal.

She tried to beat him with the crop, but he hit her hard across the face. She reeled from the shock, from the sharp, stinging pain. The stench of sweat and dirt and stale tobacco attacked her nostrils as he pinned her down, covering her with his filthy body.

"Let's see if you're 'iding a golden cunny beneath this pretty skirt."

"Get off me!" She slapped at the blackguard's fumbling fingers.

A mighty roar held her stiff with fright until she realised the cry of anger came from Benedict.

"Get your filthy hands off my wife!"

One minute the beast was writhing on top of her, the next he was hurtling through the air. Benedict dragged the man to his feet and gestured to the fiend lying unconscious on the muddy thoroughfare.

"You'll join your friend unless you tell me who sent you." Benedict's thunderous expression would terrify the devil. "Who hired you to follow us? Who hired you to attack us in the street? Tell me, damn you!"

The rogue shook his head as he gasped for breath.

"Who!" Benedict roared.

The brute pointed to his unconscious accomplice. "F-Finnigan's the only one who knows."

Hearing his name mentioned, Finnigan stirred from his forced slumber.

Benedict released the brute with the scarred lip, punched him once in the stomach and cried, "Run! Run before I change my mind and rip your head from your shoulders."

The fool didn't need to hear the command again. With no regard for the man regaining consciousness in the road, he staggered away, picking up the pace when Benedict glared and took a threatening step forward.

With only Finnigan remaining, Benedict rounded on the thug and hauled him to his feet. "I want the name of the man who hired you. The name, else I shall strike you so hard your mother won't recognise you."

Blood trickled from the fiend's nostrils, coated his swollen lips. "You'll 'ave to kill me before I squeal."

"So be it." Benedict cracked his neck and drew back his fist.

Panic settled like bony fingers around Cassandra's throat, squeezing, choking. One mistake, one missed punch, and Benedict might be the one sprawled on the ground, begging for his life. "Wait! He's not worth it. We shall find out who arranged this. I promise you."

She had made so many empty promises, broken so many vows. Indeed, she would spend her life making amends once they had solved the mystery of what happened at Lord Craven's ball. Once they'd learned the truth about Timothy's excessive spending for it most certainly gave him a motive. That said, Lord Purcell's nefarious deeds marked him as the most likely culprit.

"I want a name," Benedict growled, ignoring her plea.

Finnigan gave a mocking snort that sent blood spurting from

his nose. He spat blood and phlegm onto the muddy thoroughfare as a mark of his disdain.

"A name!" Benedict tightened his grip, forcing the rogue to gasp for breath. "Give me a damn name!" He heaved a breath, too, as he drew his fist back.

"Murray!" Finnigan covered his head with his arms. "Lord Murray hired us."

CHAPTER TEN

Benedict stood dumbfounded on the pavement. He watched Finnigan clamber to his feet, clutch his broken nose and flee the scene. Anger boiled in his blood. It had nothing to do with his injuries. Nothing to do with the attack on his person. Murray had endangered Cassandra's life, and for that, the foppish lord would pay.

Two weeks ago, Benedict might have rejoiced upon hearing of Murray's betrayal. The woman who had cast Benedict aside so easily did not deserve his sympathy. But seeing Cassandra's deflated countenance, seeing hurt swimming in her eyes, only roused feelings of pity.

Benedict caught himself. The devil on his shoulder reminded him he'd been just as callous with her during their verbal battles. Since she'd refused his suit, it was always the same with them. They hurt each other to give their own wounded hearts time to heal.

His thoughts turned back to Murray.

Did the lord love Cassandra?

Had he arranged the attack on Benedict to appease his jealousy?

There was only one way to find out.

"Are you all right?" Cassandra rushed to his side. She gripped his arm and drew him round to face her. "Good Lord." Her bottom lip trembled as she scanned his face. "You have a cut on your right cheek, a nasty bruise, too."

A thunderous roar rang in his head when he noticed the red mark on her cheek. "He hit you?" He would take Wycliff and Trent and hunt for the rogue in the rookeries.

She touched the flaming handprint with the pads of her fingers and winced. "It's nothing. Physical pain eases with time."

He cupped her cheek, was about to whisper words of comfort when she gasped upon noticing the cuts on his knuckles.

"We need to treat these wounds." She took hold of his hand and examined the split skin. "Come. We'll seek help from Mrs Crandall though you must tell me how to do that silly knock."

"It's a minor injury, nothing that requires urgent attention." Nothing that required attention at all. Still, he liked having her fuss over him. "Before we do anything else, we're calling at Murray's residence."

"Now? But you cannot pay a house call at this time of night." She drew back, unease marring her features. "Besides, is it wise to accuse a man without proof?"

After witnessing Murray's arrogant grin as he sat in his new racing curricle, Benedict sought any opportunity to berate the lord.

"Some men need to learn there are consequences to their actions. I don't believe in coincidences. A thug from the rookeries didn't just pluck Murray's name from thin air."

Cassandra pursed her lips and shook her head. "What if he issues a challenge for the insult?"

Benedict shrugged. "Then I shall name my father as my second and meet Murray at the appointed time. Though he will wish he'd picked a less lethal opponent. Let's see him race his curricle with his arm in a sling."

"Should we not concentrate our efforts on finding Foston?

He chased after those vile brutes. For all we know, he might be lying injured in an alley."

"If he is, then the other men are dead. I didn't hire the coachman for his expert driving skills."

"Evidently not. Having seen Foston pummel his opponents, I shall never complain about his erratic driving again." Her gaze softened, and she swallowed deeply. "I cannot bear to think of what might have happened had Foston not been here to help."

"They would have beaten me to death, just as Murray intended." Had Finnigan not mentioned the baron's name, Benedict's suspicions would have fallen on Lord Purcell. By all accounts, he would do anything to cause Worthen's daughter distress.

The sudden clip of footsteps on the pavement saw them both stare down the dimly lit street. Foston appeared, panting as he tried to make an apology for the delay.

"I searched the area, sir," Foston said as he came to a halt before them. The poor fellow rested his hands on his thighs as he bent forward and tried to control his ragged breathing. "But the blighters made a run for it."

Benedict patted his man on the back. "Take a moment to compose yourself. Are you hurt? Are you injured?"

"No, sir. Nothing but a few cuts and bruises."

"If you're able to drive, we're to visit Mortimer Street, near the corner of Cavendish Square."

Cassandra blinked in surprise. "You know where Lord Murray lives?"

Of course he knew. In his drunken daydreams, he'd imagined visiting the house, beating the lord and stealing away his betrothed.

"After his blatant disregard for your feelings by parading another lady around town in his curricle, I thought I might visit the mews and snap a few spokes on his new equipage."

He expected her to offer words of caution, but she shocked him by saying, "Good, then I might come with you and slash the leather seats."

They both laughed, but his cheek throbbed whenever he flexed his facial muscles.

"Come. Let us climb into the carriage and prepare for our next violent encounter. Though I suspect we've nothing to fear from a fop in a nightshirt."

Other than the dissolute bucks making a rowdy return to a house further along Mortimer Street, the place was deserted. Fog crept along the ground, rising and swirling like the reaper looking for its next victim. Soon the buildings would be hidden behind a hazy background, the people nought but dark shadows shifting through the gloom.

"Are you sure you don't want me to wipe the smears of blood off your face?" Cassandra said as Benedict assisted her descent to the pavement. "The butler will turn you away when he sees you in such a terrible state."

"I want Murray to see what we've endured. I want him to know I can beat men ten times stronger." Benedict considered her mussed hair, the dirty marks on her dress, the faint bruise on her cheek. "But perhaps you should wait in the carriage." No doubt she was ashamed of how low she'd sunk since the night of her ruination.

"You don't want me to come with you?"

There was a time when he hated being apart from her. "Are you certain you want Murray to see you looking like this?" The scandalous cut of her gown was far removed from a typical demure lady's dress.

She smoothed her hands down her skirt. "Looking like what?"

"Like a woman forced to marry beneath her station. Like a woman living a disreputable life with a rogue."

Cassandra met his gaze and raised her chin. "Regardless of how I look, I have loved every second I've spent married to you, and for that, I bear no shame. If titles were bestowed based on strength of character, you would rule this kingdom. So pray tell me how I have married beneath my station?"

Despite the cut to his face, he couldn't help but smile. "That's the nicest thing you've ever said."

"It's the truest thing I've ever said." She exhaled deeply. "Now, let us tackle this blackguard together. Let's raise Lady Murray from her comfortable bed and give her a sight to remember."

Cassandra clutched his arm, and they mounted the three steps together. Benedict hammered the brass knocker against the plate. The boom echoed through the deserted hall beyond, and so he knocked again for good measure.

After a brief wait, the sound of scurrying footsteps preceded the scraping of the bolts and the rattle of keys. The butler, looking somewhat dishevelled in his royal blue livery, opened the door a hair's breadth and peered at them through sleepy eyes.

"Mr Benedict Cavanagh to see Lord Murray." Before the butler could make an apology and send them on their way, Benedict pushed the door and thrust his foot into the gap. "Don't tell me he's not at home. Grant us entrance else I shall stand on the street and shout my accusations for all to hear."

"His l-lordship is still at his cl-club." The butler's chin wobbled, and he failed to sound convincing. Despite the obstruction, he attempted to close the door. "Call back tomorrow."

Benedict gritted his teeth. "Open the door, or there'll be hell to pay."

"Please, Fenwick," Cassandra pleaded. "We've met on many occasions, and I would not call here unless it was important." She glanced at Benedict. "I can assure you my husband will rouse the devil if he does not speak to Lord Murray."

Fenwick gave them both a disapproving stare. Before he opened his mouth to reply, Benedict grabbed the knocker and banged it a dozen times against the plate. That should wake the dandified lord from his bed.

Flustered, and not knowing what the hell to do, Fenwick beckoned them inside and closed the door. "Wait here." With his white wig cocked to one side and his stockings wrinkling at the ankles, he took to the stairs.

The creak of floorboards and the pad of footsteps above confirmed someone had risen from their bed.

"What the devil's going on?" Murray's irate voice reached Benedict's ears. "It sounds as though the damned cavalry are beating their way inside."

"You have visitors, my lord."

"Visitors? At this ungodly hour?"

Murray was unlike most hot-blooded young men of the *ton*. He did not venture to gaming hells or visit brothels. He did not entertain a mistress, or drink to excess. Indeed, he would be a perfect example of a respectable lord, were it not for his excessive spending.

Fenwick took to whispering, though Murray was keen to let the world know of his annoyance. "Then send them away."

The butler muttered something else, and Murray huffed in frustration.

The lord appeared moments later wearing a burgundy silk robe and matching nightcap. It took Benedict every effort to keep the smirk from his face. But remembering the moment the thug slapped Cassandra brought his rage surging back.

"What the devil do you—" Murray came to an abrupt halt halfway down the stairs and stared at them incredulously. "Good Lord. Has there been an accident?" He hurried down the remaining steps, concern etched on his brow.

"An accident?" Benedict gritted his teeth. "You know damn well what has occurred."

Murray's eyes widened. "I haven't the first clue what you're talking about. Come. Let me call my housekeeper to tend to your wounds."

"We were set upon by four thugs." Benedict clenched his fists at his sides, relishing the stinging pain as it reminded him of the beating. "They commanded my carriage and were waiting on Theobolds Road. Thankfully, my coachman possesses a skill for pugilism. Still, that didn't prevent one of them hitting Cassandra."

The lord's gaze darted to Cassandra's face, though numerous times it dipped to the low-cut neckline of her gown.

"And you think I had something to do with this?" The tassel on Murray's cap flicked back and forth as he shook his head. "You think I would condone a man hitting a woman? Surely not."

Benedict stepped forward, and Murray clutched the lapels of his robe and shuffled back.

"Finnigan said you hired them to attack me." A thug wouldn't know the significance of the name, wouldn't know of the man's motive. A thug cared only for the money. "He named you. Do you expect me to believe someone else by the name of Lord Murray paid men to pummel me in the street?"

Murray's jaw dropped. It took seconds before he formed a word. "But that's ridiculous. I wouldn't know how to hire ruffians from the rookeries."

"I didn't say they were from the rookeries."

"Well, isn't it obvious? Besides, I'm grateful you married Cassandra. I couldn't wed a woman embroiled in a scandal."

Cassandra inhaled deeply but said nothing.

The old feelings of mistrust and doubt surfaced. Had Cassandra lied to him? "You ended the betrothal? You told Cassandra you couldn't marry her?"

The lord grimaced. "The situation was impossible. Cassandra knew that. Love, and respect for my position saw her make the ultimate sacrifice."

"So she released you from your obligation?"

"Well, yes, though she had little choice in the matter. As I said, her sense of duty—"

"I released you because I don't love you," Cassandra blurted. "I never have. And while I respected your position, I released you because any man who drinks port at his club while the woman he supposedly loves faces her worst nightmare is not a man I would want for a husband."

Murray seemed confused. "Of course you loved me. Why the devil would you agree to marry me otherwise?"

"I could ask you the same question," she countered. "We both know the answer. For power and position. Out of a misguided sense of guilt and duty. To keep our obsessive parents happy."

The lord puffed out his chest. "I'll not have you speak ill of my mother. It's not obsessive to care for one's child."

Benedict had reached his limit of tolerance and so bellowed, "Admit you hired those men to beat me!"

Murray jumped back in shock at the sudden outburst. The stomping of footsteps on the boards upstairs left the man quivering like a boy awaiting the school bully.

"Now do you see what you've done?" Murray's gaze lingered painfully on the stairs. He turned to Cassandra. "I told my mother I was the one who ended our betrothal. There's no need to inform her otherwise."

Curse the saints!

And to think Worthen wanted his daughter to marry this browbeaten, spineless excuse for a lord.

A figure shrouded in a white wrapper and frilly cap appeared at the top of the stairs. Lady Murray descended with forthright steps, her back as rigid as her opinions. She stared at them as if they were street urchins come begging for scraps.

"What's the meaning of this?" Lady Murray stared down her pointed nose. "You're accosted and abused in your own home, and you didn't think to wake me?"

"It's nothing, Mother." The lord's voice lacked the power he'd attempted to display earlier. "A case of mistaken identity, that is all."

The matron glanced at the butler who had taken to lingering

at the end of the hall. "Fetch the watchman, Fenwick. Let him remove these despicable beings."

Benedict had dealt with this level of disdain many times before. "Yes, fetch the watchman, Fenwick. I wish to accuse Lord Murray of a crime. The marks on my face will act as evidence." And yet a feeling in his gut told him Murray was innocent of any wrongdoing.

"A crime?" the matron scoffed. "Don't be ridiculous. Timothy is an upstanding member of society, not a whoremonger willing to marry a harlot." She smirked as her beady eyes turned to Cassandra. "Your father must be so proud."

Cassandra straightened. Her face held the same determination he'd noted when she'd walloped the thug with the riding crop. "Well, you would know what it's like to have a child who doesn't live up to your expectations. How much longer do you think you can hide Timothy's lavish spending? Has he lied about the cost of his new racing curricle?"

The matron blanched.

Terror marred Murray's countenance. "It's not new. I purchased it for an excellent price from a debt-ridden merchant who needed funds." From the wobble in his voice, it was obviously a lie.

"I don't know what nonsense you've concocted in your head, gel," the matron began, "but do not think to come here and throw your absurd accusations."

Cassandra shrugged. "Terrible things happen to respectable people. Unless we hear the truth from your son's lips, we will be forced to spread ugly rumours. It might interest Miss Pendleton to learn that you're on the brink of bankruptcy."

Lady Murray's cheeks ballooned. "Why, you devious little minx. Wait until—"

"Do not dare threaten me. Wait until we inform Tregarth that your son hired men to beat his son to death. Only a fool would risk the earl's wrath. And your son is most definitely a fool."

While Benedict watched the scene with glowing admiration for his wife, Murray threw his arms in the air in protest.

"How many times must I tell you? I know nothing about hiring ruffians from the rookeries. Someone wishes you to believe it was me to steer you away from the real culprit."

Benedict sensed some truth in the lord's words. "Then tell me, who else has a motive?"

"What about Purcell?" Murray suggested. "He despises Lord Worthen. Many times he warned me against marrying Cassandra. Perhaps he hired the men and gave my name to shift the blame."

It was a possibility. Thankfully Benedict knew of a man with the right connections to discover the truth.

Lady Murray nodded. "Lord Purcell will go to great lengths to seek his revenge on Lord Worthen. He whispered his vile words in my ear, too. After consuming copious amounts of brandy at Lord Craven's ball, he told anyone willing to listen that he had plans to make your father pay."

Purcell knew about the demimonde's riotous gatherings.

Purcell had spoken to Mrs Crandall of his devious plots. And so was he attempting to throw them off the scent by blaming Murray?

"Purcell left the ball early," Lady Murray added. "Indeed, he disappeared long before your father came from the card room looking for you."

CHAPTER ELEVEN

"What shall we do about Lord Purcell?" Cassandra relaxed back in the carriage and watched Benedict as he rummaged around in the leather satchel he'd taken from the storage box beneath the velvet seat. "We can hardly accuse him of attempted murder based on nothing more than Lord Murray's suspicions."

Benedict took a length of bandage and wrapped it around his right hand, covering the split skin on his knuckles. "I'm tired of following false leads. Scarlett is acquainted with a man named Dermot Flannery who runs a gaming hell called The Silver Serpent. I shall send word to Wycliff in the morning and ask him to contact Flannery in the hope he might discover who hired the thugs."

"Do ruffians from the rookeries frequent gaming hells?"

"Flannery will call in a debt and should have no problem discovering the information, given that we provide him with reasonable descriptions."

An image of the beastly fiend who attacked her flashed into her mind. The terrifying sight sent a shiver rippling to her toes. "The man who hit me had a jagged scar running across his top lip. There was something feral about his black eyes, the gold flecks conveying a certain savagery. He was missing numerous teeth, though his incisors were longer, sharper than the average man's."

Benedict muttered a curse as he tied a knot in the bandage and flexed his fist. "While Finnigan may not be my attacker's real name, he'll have purple plums for eyes come the morning and should be easy to identify."

"You certainly gave him a good beating."

The Benedict Cavanagh she used to know didn't brawl with men in the street. He did not visit houses of ill-repute or threaten the blue bloods of the aristocracy. And yet she found him more irresistible than ever. Indeed, with Timothy's fear of his mother and his foppish ways, how had she ever imagined marrying the lord? That said, she had been coerced into accepting the proposal.

As if reading her thoughts, Benedict said, "Tell me. Did you speak the truth when you said you've never loved Lord Murray?"

Embarrassed that she had followed her father's will and not her own, she glanced out of the window into the darkness. "I liked him enough to think we could create a life together. But no, I was never in love with him."

Silence descended though she could feel the power of Benedict's stare scorching her skin.

"There's something shifty about Murray, something I don't trust. Men dominated by their mothers often find secret outlets for self-expression. Hence his excessive spending."

She found the courage to meet Benedict's gaze. "Like me, Timothy has learned to hide behind a mask. Life is bearable if he abides by his mother's rules."

Benedict sat forward. "Is that why you threw away a chance of happiness with me? You *were* happy when we were together?" He sounded apprehensive. "You didn't fake the laughter, fake the caring gestures and loving words?"

She swallowed past the hard lump in her throat. "You're the

only person in the world who truly knows me. Even now, I feel as if I'm floundering in a turbulent sea, bobbing between the past and the present."

"The past is lost to us. We were innocent and young and believed love could conquer prejudices. Neither of us are the same people. Too much has happened. Too much has changed."

A mild panic fluttered in her chest. "Are you saying we will never feel the way we used to?" Oh, she couldn't bear to think he might never love her again.

"Honestly, I have no notion what the future holds. But we're talking as a husband and wife should. We're not attacking each other at every given opportunity." His gaze dipped to her mouth. "And when I kiss you, all our problems seem to fade away."

"We used to steal every spare moment to press our lips together." They would never have been able to sit alone in a closed carriage and not partake in a little amorous activity. But while they would have held each other in a tender embrace, now she imagined they would tear at each other's clothes, desperate to reignite the connection.

His blue eyes flashed hot as his gaze slid down the length of her body. "Perhaps we should kiss more often. After all, you are my wife."

Parched for his affection, she said, "It seems like a perfectly reasonable thing for a married couple to do." And she would do anything to feel close to him again. Anything.

Without further discussion, he crossed the carriage and dropped into the seat beside her. He captured her chin between his blood-stained fingers and closed his mouth over hers in an achingly slow kiss.

Desire coiled in her core. She wanted to strip off his clothes, straddle him, take him into her body and never let go. While every inch of her thrummed with the need to consume him, she tempered her emotions as her tongue caressed his in an intimate dance.

He was right.

They were far from the same people.

The kiss was intense. A desperate need clung to every movement of their mouths. Years of yearning echoed in every throaty moan. The hunger ravaging her body feasted on the essence of the man she used to love, might still love if only she could push aside thoughts of guilt and gratitude. If only she didn't loathe herself for being weak, for making the wrong decision.

Good heavens!

Here she was again, wavering between the past and the present. This moment was all that mattered—the feel of his hot mouth, the heat radiating from his skin. She reached up and cupped his unblemished cheek, deepening the kiss, conveying every ounce of affection she held for this man.

When the carriage rumbled to a halt, she almost groaned in protest.

Benedict dragged his lips from hers. "I think I prefer the way you kiss me now." The impassioned look in his eyes sent pulses shooting to her sex. "There's something raw about the way you devour my mouth. Something wild and untempered."

"Trust me. If you think I've had tutorage in the art, you're mistaken." She was still the same innocent girl who knew hardly anything about relations with men. "I've never kissed another man the way I kiss you."

A laugh escaped him. "It was not an accusation, but an observation."

"Oh. Perhaps you sense a need in me to make things right between us." That wasn't what she meant, but how could she say she lusted after her husband a mere week since she should have been marrying someone else?

"Make things right?" He straightened, his mood shifting. "I don't want to spend every moment wondering if your actions stem from a sense of duty or a desire to make amends." The passion in his eyes dimmed.

"And I don't want to spend every moment wondering if you still resent me for rejecting you all those years ago."

"Forget about the past. Just be yourself." Frustration rang in his tone. "Tease me. Scold me. Laugh at me."

A chuckle escaped her as an image burst into her mind. "So you want me to hurl conkers at you when you're not looking?"

The most alluring smile she had ever seen formed on his lips. "Yes, and like last time I shall chase you, pin you down and relish the feel of your body writhing beneath mine."

Heat flamed between her thighs as she recalled every divine sensation. "Then you must do the same. Be yourself. Kiss me when the mood takes you. Sleep with me." *Love me*, she added silently. *Please learn to love me again.* "Let me be your wife."

He studied her, warring emotions clashing in his handsome blue eyes.

"I don't want to sleep alone tonight, Benedict." She had spent a lifetime on her own. "Surely spending more time together will only help to nurture our relationship."

He remained silent for a moment before his gaze dropped to the swell of her breasts. "We both need to bathe. It's a little late to expect the servants to heat water for more than one bathtub. Let's start there and see where the mood takes us."

Despite a sudden pang of nerves at the thought of stripping naked, she smiled. "You can relax in the tub first while I wash the blood from your face and hands." Having felt the sheer power of his muscular physique, she longed to see what he looked like without clothes.

An excitable energy vibrated in the air as Benedict assisted her out of the carriage and into the house. He calmed Mrs Rampling's concerns over the cut to his cheek and then fired instructions. In less than an hour, Cassandra was alone with him in her bedchamber, a bathtub of steaming water sitting before the roaring fire.

She watched in awe as Benedict stripped off his coat, waistcoat and cravat. She watched every sleek movement until he stood in nothing but a shirt and breeches.

He padded over to her, his sinful grin promising something

wicked. “My knuckles hurt. Perhaps you might help divest me of the last two garments.”

“With pleasure.” With trembling yet eager fingers, she tugged his shirt free from his breeches. She should have lifted the garment over his head, but the urge to touch his bare skin proved too tempting to resist.

Benedict sucked in a sharp breath when her hands settled on his waist.

“Your body is so hard,” she whispered, running her fingers over the solid muscles in his abdomen. “So hard.”

He reached under his shirt, covered her hand and slid it down to the fall of his breeches. “So hard, I’m finding it immensely difficult to keep from throwing you onto the bed and thrusting past your maidenhead.”

Her fingers brushed over the solid length of his erection.

Good Lord!

Her heart raced so fast she could hardly breathe. The sweet ache between her thighs controlled her thoughts. Indeed, having Benedict Cavanagh between her legs was her only motivation.

He cupped her nape and kissed her in the wild, reckless way of a man consumed with raging lust. With his other hand, he continued to help her massage his manhood which grew thicker, more impressive by the second.

The temperature in the room soared.

Her pulse increased at such a rapid rate she became dizzy. Dizzy with desire. Dizzy with the knowledge she would finally take the only man she had ever wanted into her body.

Benedict broke contact and panted to catch his breath. “I know I said we should bathe. I know I said we would see where the mood takes us, but the need to be inside you is driving me insane.”

“I want you, too.” Oh, she had wanted him for so long. She rubbed his erection in the hope he would realise how much. “I know nothing of the intimacies shared in the bedroom, but I don’t want to wait, Benedict.”

They needed no further inducement.

Benedict fumbled with the fall of his breeches.

"Hurry." She gathered her skirts up to her waist as they both tumbled onto the bed.

She expected to feel his weight pressing her down into the mattress, but he knelt between her thighs and kissed her sex with the same fervent passion he had her mouth.

Need outweighed her embarrassment.

Need that soon turned to begging.

"Oh, God! Benedict. Don't stop." She wanted to grasp his hair and rub against his wet mouth, but he was hidden beneath her skirt like a rake pleasuring his mistress in a secluded corner of a ballroom.

With every caress of Benedict's tongue, lust's coil wound tighter. So tight she came apart with a violent shudder and a keen cry, pleasure exploding inside with all the wonder of fireworks at Vauxhall.

She clutched the coverlet. "*Benedict!*" A hum resonated in her throat as she soared on the magnificent heights of her release.

Benedict appeared from under the mound of material. Despite being clothed, she imagined his sweat-soaked muscles rippling beneath his shirt. He tugged his breeches down low on his hips, took hold of his manhood—thick and hard with the evidence of his arousal—pumped the solid shaft and then positioned himself at her entrance.

"Are you sure you want to do this?" He looked at her through the sapphire-blue haze of his desire. A vision she had seen once before when he had touched her intimately during one of their secret midnight liaisons.

"More sure than I've been about anything my entire life." She had dreamt of this moment many times, yet the reality of being close to him exceeded every expectation.

"I'll be as mindful as I can under the circumstances. Tell me if it proves too uncomfortable to bear."

She swallowed deeply and nodded.

The first nudge of his manhood breeching her entrance caused a quickening in her core. Pure pleasure, not pain. When he pushed inside her another inch, her body stretched to accommodate him as if they were destined to be a perfect fit.

"This part was always going to be difficult," she said when he hesitated, when he closed his eyes and inhaled a deep breath. "My desire to be your wife in more than name will override any discomfort."

"You were always meant for me," he said, opening his eyes and meeting her gaze.

"Always." She gripped his hips in encouragement, urging him to claim her as he should have done five years ago.

He bent his head and slanted his mouth over hers. The kiss lacked the fervent urgency that came with rampant desire, was more a teasing glimpse of the soul-deep satisfaction to come.

A husky hum resonated in his throat as he pushed a little deeper. She became so lost in the mating of their tongues, in the earthy scent of his skin, in how wonderful it felt to connect with him in this primitive dance, that she almost forgot he was to claim her virginity.

The final thrust snatched the air from her lungs. She dragged her mouth from his on a gasp. Not because it felt painful—a little uncomfortable, yes—but knowing she belonged to Benedict now sent a wave of euphoria crashing through her body.

"God, Cassandra," he panted, holding himself still for a moment. "Everything about this feels so right. So damn good."

She had never doubted it for a second.

"I'm your wife now, in every way that matters." Not in the most important way. Somehow they had to learn to love each other again. "We are as one, Benedict. The way it should have been."

"Yes," he breathed, as he withdrew so slowly she ached from the emptiness.

He fixed her with his intense gaze, rolled his hips and filled her full again and again. Oh, the pleasure, the sheer bliss, was beyond anything she could have imagined.

"I'm not hurting you?"

"No." He had never hurt her, never could. She caressed his back, found the courage to push her hands below the waistband of his breeches to grip his buttocks and urge him to continue this delicious dance. "Again," she panted when he withdrew. "I need you inside me, Benedict." *For always. Forever.*

Her words seemed to rouse a lusty hunger in him, and he increased the pace, thrusting hard and long, the audible slapping a celebration of their union.

"Don't stop." Her pulse drummed a potent rhythm, too. She wished they were naked so she might feel the heat from his body, the dampness coating his skin.

He clutched her buttocks and pumped harder—wild and reckless. But then he slowed. "*Cassandra*." His head fell back as he jerked his hips and gave a groan of satisfaction.

Panting for breath, he collapsed on top of her, pinning her to the bed. Never had being squashed felt so divine.

"Forgive me," he breathed. "I intended to withdraw as we haven't discussed the matter of children, but you're my wife, and I lost my head for a moment."

He was still buried inside her, and she wished they could remain this way for eternity. "Nothing would please me more than bearing your child. You're right, we're married and shall find a way through the uncertainties."

He bent his head, claimed her mouth and kissed her so deeply, so slowly, the familiar ache returned. The sensation made her writhe against him, searching for a way to prolong their joining.

Benedict drew back from the kiss and eased himself out of her body. "We should bathe before the water is too cold."

"You bathe first." She looked at the cut on his cheek, at the blood smeared on his face. She had almost forgotten about the attack, almost forgotten her thighs must bear the claret smears of her virginity, too.

Benedict hadn't forgotten.

"Come, the warm water will prove soothing. If there's room perhaps we might bathe together."

She would make room. What could be more erotic than washing with her husband?

Somehow they squeezed into the tub. The rug near the hearth absorbed the water spilling over the rim. Benedict draped his legs over the edges to give her more room, soaped his hands and washed her breasts as she lay back against his chest. Every brush of his fingers across her nipples fired the ache deep in her core.

"Tomorrow," he said when she pressed her buttocks back against his erection. Wedged together in the tub, she couldn't help but notice. "After your first time, it's too soon for me to ravage your body again."

So why did he continue to massage her breasts with sensual strokes?

The answer became abundantly clear when he slid his hand down into the water and began rubbing her sex.

Now she knew why Mrs Crandall was desperate to bed him. His fingers worked magic. They slipped back and forth in the soapy water, each skilled caress drawing her closer to her release.

"But your knuckles, they must hurt," she said, but that didn't stop her moaning, jerking her hips and writhing against his hand.

"I never do anything unless I want to," he said, pressing his lips to the beating pulse in her neck as he plucked her strings like a famed maestro. "That's the luxury of illegitimacy. Now relax and think about the next time I'm thrusting so deep into your body you cannot help but pant my name."

Heavens above! She came apart the moment the erotic vision entered her head. Waves of pleasure burst wildly from her core. "Oh, yes." How she wished that moment was now.

"That's it, love. Tell me how good it feels. Tell me how you long to have me inside you."

"I can think about nothing else." She would offer herself to him again and again. She could make love to him a thousand times, and it would never be enough.

"Good. As I expect we shall do this often."

"You will hear no complaints from me." She sagged back against his chest and closed her eyes.

They must have both fallen asleep for the water was cold when he stirred and shook her shoulder. She sat up, and he climbed out of the tub and padded naked across the room to retrieve a towel. *Magnificent* was the only way to describe his firm buttocks, thick thighs and broad shoulders.

"It's late. You need a good night's sleep," he said, drying his body before offering his hand to assist her from the tub. "We'll need our wits at Tregarth's ball tomorrow evening if we hope to confront Purcell."

"I'm sure your father arranged the ball just to prove a point." No one in the *ton* would refuse an invitation to the earl's soirée. Indeed, she was looking forward to seeing Rosamund and Sybil and was intrigued to hear more about Sybil's developments with Mr Daventry.

"The hypocrites will arrive in their droves." He began drying her body with the linen towel, and it took every effort to concentrate on the conversation. "No one will dare mention the incident in Hyde Park whilst in my father's house."

"And will the Wycliffs and the Trents be there?"

"Everyone important to me receives an invitation." He took her hand and drew her towards the bed. "There's no need to wear a nightgown."

The desperate need to ask why came upon her, but fear of spoiling such a wonderful evening rendered her mute.

Benedict smiled as if he had access to her thoughts. "Do you mind if I share your bed tonight?"

She swallowed past the sudden rush of excitement, past the

warm feeling glowing in her chest. "You're my husband. Why would I mind?" But the need to speak from the heart saw her add, "There's nothing I would like more than to be close to you."

He inclined his head, pulled back the coverlet and waited for her to slip beneath the sheets. He joined her in bed, kissed her in the sinful yet affectionate way that tugged at the muscles deep inside. Then he relaxed back on the pillow and fell asleep within minutes.

Fascinated, she hugged her pillow and watched the soft rise and fall of his chest, studied every facet of the man she had loved for as long as she could remember. The man she still loved to the depths of her soul.

CHAPTER TWELVE

The Earl of Tregarth did nothing in small measure. Benedict surveyed his father's opulent ballroom and smiled. Expensive Italian chandeliers reflected the candlelight to a greater degree. Lavish paintings in ornate gilt frames decorated the vibrant burgundy walls. The orchestra—renowned throughout Europe for their skill and expertise—only played for the king and a select few granted a royal decree. The earl enjoyed reminding the members of the aristocracy of his wealth and power. Not because he thought himself superior or because he sought gratification. No. His father's motivation stemmed from making life more bearable for Benedict.

Cassandra touched Benedict lightly on the arm. "Your father has spared no expense this evening. The ice sculptures are the best I have ever seen." She pointed to Cupid equipped with his bow. "Like the ancient sculptures one finds in museums."

"My father hires Fausto Farino whenever he wishes to beat the lesser members of society back into place."

"There are few who can afford Signore Farino's extortionate fee."

"Hence the reason Tregarth employs him to organise his

gatherings. And to remind those here that most of my father's wealth shall be mine one day."

Cassandra cast him a sidelong glance and smiled. "It must be comforting to know your father loves you, loves you more than anything else."

A man born on the wrong side of the blanket took nothing for granted. Other than his friends, his father was the only person who had never failed him.

"Yes," he acknowledged. His father's love gave him the confidence to go out into the world, to take risks, to make mistakes. "It certainly eases the burden of illegitimacy."

With some trepidation—for he knew how his friends would react upon seeing the evidence of the brutal attack on Theobolds Road—Benedict escorted Cassandra down the stairs to join Wycliff, Trent and the men's wives.

Benedict had barely taken a breath when Trent grabbed his arm and glared at his cheek. "What the devil's happened to your face?"

Benedict pressed the pads of his fingers to the cut and winced. "Someone hired four thugs to attack us as we left Mrs Crandall's abode last night. But lower your voice. I mean to avoid my father else he'll be hellbent on revenge."

Wycliff's dark gaze hardened. "Why the blazes didn't you mention your injuries when you sent word asking for Flannery's assistance? When you gave a name and a description and said the men were from the rookeries, I assumed it had something to do with Cassandra's kidnapping. And why the hell did you go to Mrs Crandall's house alone? The woman is as devious as the devil."

Benedict was about to answer when Scarlett sucked in a sharp breath. She reached out and gently brushed aside Cassandra's ringlets. "Your cheek is bruised, too."

"It's nothing, just a slight swelling from a hard slap. I couldn't stand there and let those brutes beat my husband."

All four of his friends looked on incredulously.

"Cassandra attacked one with a riding crop." Admiration for his wife's actions rang in Benedict's tone. "Foston dealt with the other two, leaving me alone with the thug who goes by the name of Finnigan."

"After receiving your note, I met with Flannery," Wycliff said. "The name was unfamiliar, but he will speak to his contacts on the streets and inform me should he learn more about the men you described."

"Finnigan said Lord Murray hired them."

"Murray!" Trent whispered through gritted teeth. "The damn coward. He's here somewhere. I shall take him to a quiet corner of the garden and throttle a confession from his lying lips."

"We visited Murray at home and dragged him from his bed." A vision of the lord wearing his jaunty nightcap made Benedict smile. "The man insists he's innocent."

"And you believe him?" Wycliff snorted. "Give me a moment alone with Murray, too, and we'll soon get to the truth."

"I don't know what to believe." Benedict told them about Mrs Crandall's revelation regarding Murray's financial situation. "Murray has no reason to hurt me. If he arranged Cassandra's ruination, he would have used the attack to throw the blame elsewhere. He could have told Finnigan to say Purcell had hired them."

"A fair point," Wycliff admitted. "Or the man is so stupid he didn't think you would ask. So, you want Flannery to find out who hired the thugs?"

"Indeed."

"That still leaves Murray in the frame for kidnapping."

"Lord Murray has been fawning over Miss Pendleton from the moment she arrived tonight," Verity added. "Having a reason not to marry Cassandra has given him the freedom to pursue a lady who possesses a substantial dowry."

Scarlett gave a coy smile. "Then perhaps I might whisper a warning in Miss Pendleton's ear when she retires to the ladies' room. Though one would hope the woman isn't naive enough to suppose he holds some affection for her."

"If I'm not mistaken, is that not them dancing the waltz?" Verity gestured to the foppish lord and the lady who, in Benedict's opinion, paled in comparison to Cassandra.

"Some men have no shame." Scarlett tutted. "Cassandra, I know you won't think so now, but you should thank the person who left you in Hyde Park and sent Benedict the letter."

Cassandra looked at Benedict in the same heated way she had when they'd satisfied their lustful cravings. Although *satisfied* was hardly the right word. Desire for his wife continually simmered beneath the surface.

"On the contrary, I'm more thankful than you could ever know," Cassandra said, radiant in her happiness. "Indeed, the more time we spend searching for the villain, the less it matters."

"Discovering the truth is important, else mistrust eats away at you like a deadly poison," Verity said somewhat dramatically. "The truth will bring closure."

"How will we ever find the truth when I cannot remember a thing about that night?"

"You must remember something," Scarlett countered. "Something before you became unwell. There must have been a moment when the room suddenly felt different."

"Try to think about what you do remember," Verity suggested, rather excited about the prospect, "not what you don't. Come, let us move closer to the terrace doors. The music is so loud it is difficult to concentrate."

They did as Verity suggested and found a quiet spot near a fake blossom tree with flowers of white silk, away from the wandering magician and those cooing over the ice sculptures.

"Now, what do you remember?" Verity said as if she worked for an inspector at Bow Street. "Even the most insignificant things might be important." One almost expected her to pluck a pencil from behind her ear and ask if anyone had a pocketbook.

A frown marred Cassandra's brow. Her vision grew distant as

she scanned the crowded ballroom and watched the elegant couples circling the floor. When she looked up at the chandelier, at the candles flaming so brightly it was blinding, she blinked rapidly.

"Murray had gone to fetch me a glass of orgeat lemonade." Cassandra paused and pursed her lips. "He was gone for a while. I remember joking that a lady might die if she waited for him to quench her thirst."

"Did he say what kept him?" Wycliff asked suspiciously.

"No. But when I woke the next morning in the park, I could taste the sweet remnants of the lemonade. That was the last drink to pass my lips."

Benedict muttered a curse. He slipped a comforting arm around Cassandra's waist, an action that drew a look of surprise from Trent. "What were you doing while Murray went to fetch refreshments?" She had already given him an account of the evening, but it might prompt one of his friends to ask a different question.

"Hmm. Sybil had gone to the card room. Apparently, one learns a wealth of information while watching those at play. I told her to inform me when my father took his leave."

"Why?" Trent asked bluntly.

"Because he gives me tasks that involve prying into other people's affairs. I often hide in the retiring room when I know he is on the prowl."

Wycliff rubbed his chin in thoughtful contemplation. "And did you ever discover a secret that might give someone cause to hurt you?"

"No. Never. Mostly I lied to my father, told him men prefer to make idle conversation while dancing."

Silence ensued, though the room thrummed with the hum of music, lively conversation and light laughter.

"I couldn't find Rosamund."

"Miss Rosamund Fox," Benedict explained. "Sir William's daughter."

Trent snorted. "Perhaps she was searching the dark closets looking for her father."

"Sir William is renowned for conducting liaisons in confined spaces," Benedict informed his wife. "There's something about one's inability to breathe he finds fascinating."

"Oh!" Cassandra looked shocked and bemused. "I spoke to Lady Murray, who lamented her son's lax attitude to agreeing on a wedding date. She assured me he would decide soon."

Something about the whole situation proved confounding. If Murray needed money, why not marry quickly to secure Cassandra's dowry? Unless he had other reasons for wanting to delay. Perhaps he had fallen in love with Miss Pendleton, had been looking for a way to break his betrothal to Cassandra without her father suing for breach of promise.

The more Benedict considered the only two suspects in the investigation—Purcell and Murray—the more convinced he was both men were guilty.

"When Lord Murray returned," Cassandra continued, "I drank the lemonade, though mentioned it tasted bitter."

"And what was Murray's response?" Trent asked.

"He made a derogatory comment about Lord Craven, about his staff being incapable, and then we danced the waltz before he left me again to go in search of his mother."

"Evidently the lemonade contained the substance used to render you unconscious," Wycliff said. "Can you remember feeling the effects before your world plunged into darkness?"

Cassandra fell silent for a moment. "Dancing made me tired and dizzy, my limbs heavy. I went to sit down and then Rosamund appeared. She offered to accompany me to the retiring room, but I insisted on going alone, though I barely remember the conversation. Indeed, I remember little else after that."

Once again, silence ensued while they absorbed the information.

"If I'm correct," Scarlett began, "the retiring room in Lord Craven's house has double doors leading out to the terrace."

"Yes, though the curtains were drawn and there was a series of dressing screens blocking the exit. I remember because I had visited the room earlier that evening."

Wycliff sighed. "Though loath to point out the obvious, I'd place my bet on Murray. He's the only one with motive and opportunity."

"You forget that a groom saw Purcell bundle a woman into his carriage on the night in question," Trent said. "Perhaps Purcell distracted Murray on his way back to the ballroom and poured a tincture into the lemonade."

Benedict nodded. "We know Purcell left the ball early."

"And what about Murray?" Wycliff focused his attention on Cassandra. "What time did he leave? Can anyone vouch for his whereabouts after you disappeared?"

Cassandra's eyes widened. "I never thought to ask." A blush stained her cheeks. "I suppose I thought him incapable of committing such a heinous crime."

"Our lives have been somewhat hectic since we married," Benedict interjected in her defence. *Hectic* was a gross understatement. "We've barely had a minute to breathe." An image of her panting beneath him sent a lightning bolt of lust shooting to his loins.

"Then determining if Murray has an alibi must be paramount," Wycliff said, "although that still doesn't mean Murray wasn't involved."

Trent squared his shoulders. "Then let us beat the truth from the man. Indeed, we could bring this matter to a swift conclusion with the right amount of pressure."

Verity gave a frustrated sigh. "If our dealings with the Brethren taught us anything, it's that one should expect the unexpected. Whoever devised the plan to ruin Cassandra was rather meticulous in the details. Forgive me, but Lord Murray seems incapable of managing his diary."

A footman approached carrying a tray laden with flutes of champagne. They all took one. The men downed the contents. The ladies sipped their drinks while lost in thought.

"So, we must make a plan of action." Scarlett cast her attention over the group. "Damian will visit Dermot Flannery and make enquiries into the brutes who attacked you. Lawrence will revisit Lord Craven's groom and press for a more detailed description of the lady bundled into Purcell's carriage. Purcell's coachman must have brought his carriage round to the private mews at a specified time."

Benedict inclined his head in agreement. "Whoever kidnapped Cassandra must have left via the mews." A man didn't walk out of a grand house with an unconscious woman flung over his shoulder. "We need to know who else used the mews that night." People made a discreet exit for a variety of reasons.

A mischievous smile played at the corners of Trent's mouth. "I shall attend to the matter first thing in the morning."

"And I shall tackle the issue of Murray's alibi." Benedict would start by questioning those people he knew were in attendance.

"What shall I do?" Cassandra seemed more than eager for a role in this plan. "I could speak to Miss Pendleton. Perhaps Lord Murray made promises while we were still betrothed."

"An excellent idea." Scarlett smiled. "I've heard that revisiting the scene of a crime often rouses suppressed memories. Perhaps you and Benedict should follow the route from Lord Craven's ball to Hyde Park when you leave here tonight."

Benedict would try anything if it meant finding the culprit. Only then could they move on with their lives, regain some semblance of normality.

"The retiring room here is somewhat similar to the one Lord Craven allocated for his guests. Perhaps a visit might spark a memory." Scarlett was a fountain of useful suggestions.

Cassandra finished her champagne and handed Benedict her

glass. "Then we shall go now. I should like to have at least one waltz with my husband before the night is through and cannot give him my undivided attention when my mind is plagued by the past."

Benedict placed their empty flutes on a passing footman's tray, as did his friends, before capturing Cassandra's hand and pressing a kiss to her gloved knuckles. "I shall go in search of those who might remember Murray's movements that night. Shall we agree to meet here in half an hour?"

Their gazes locked. The twinkle of desire in Cassandra's eyes fed his own craving. Indeed, he wasn't sure if he could wait until they were home to make love to her again.

"Perfect. And I shall look forward to our first dance together as husband and wife."

He touched her upper arm just below the puffed sleeve of her blue gown and stroked his thumb back and forth. "We seem to fall into a natural rhythm when we're together."

Her cheeks flushed. "Then the dance promises to be more than pleasing."

He smiled. But as she moved away from him to join Scarlett and Verity, a sudden panic took hold. "Like any protective husband, I pray you'll be careful."

Wycliff cleared his throat. "May I ask a question before you venture to the ladies' room?"

"Of course." Cassandra smiled.

"What did your father do when it was time to leave Lord Craven's ball and he couldn't find you?"

Lips pursed, Cassandra looked to the ceiling. After a brief time, she said, "Honestly, I don't know. He's not a man who converses civilly. But he would have left without saying a word, out of fear of ruining my reputation."

"And what did he say when Benedict brought you home?"

Benedict was curious as to Wycliff's train of thought. "Worthen didn't stop ranting from the moment we entered the study. He blamed me, had convinced himself I was responsible." The earl had been a tad more colourful with his words.

"My father believes we planned my disgrace so I could marry Benedict. Someone told him we were in love, and he suspected we'd eloped. But when Benedict initially refused to marry me, it put paid to his theory."

"I see."

"When he left the ball, did your father call at Benedict's house in Jermyn Street?" Trent enquired. "That would be the obvious place to look if he suspected you were together."

Cassandra stared blankly.

Benedict frowned. That hadn't occurred to him either. Since taking Cassandra for his bride, his mind was somewhat addled. "No. Mrs Rampling would have informed me had Worthen called."

"Well, perhaps it's of no consequence. Indeed, who can say what goes through a distraught father's mind." Wycliff turned to Scarlett. "I shall remain here until you've finished in the retiring room." His dark gaze slid over his wife's body. "Perhaps you might like to waltz with your husband, too."

Scarlett arched a brow. "You know I would."

They watched their wives cut through the throng and disappear into the crowd.

As soon as the ladies were out of view, Trent said, "Do you not find Worthen's actions rather odd?"

"Everything about the pompous lord defies understanding."

Wycliff folded his arms across his chest. "If Worthen truly believed you were together, then your house should have been his first port of call. If he truly believed you'd eloped, then surely he would have taken to the Great North Road. Checked the coaching inns en route."

"The earl spouts vile nonsense most of the time." Benedict had heard enough over the years to close his ears to it now. "He derives power from hurling false accusations." Which was why he had not given the matter another thought.

"So who told the earl you and Cassandra were in love? Someone out to make trouble?"

Benedict shrugged. "I've every faith Worthen concocted the tale. Or perhaps the person who had me arrive at the Serpentine before Purcell and his ilk sought to stir the cooking pot. Whoever it was based their opinion on mere supposition."

What other explanation was there?

No one knew Benedict's inner thoughts.

No one knew he had never stopped loving Cassandra Mills.

CHAPTER THIRTEEN

"Your mother is looking for you, my dear." Scarlett cupped the elbow of the only young lady using the retiring room and guided her towards the door. "Indeed, I am certain Lady Murray said her son wishes to dance with you."

The lady's innocent eyes widened, and she batted her lashes before hurrying out into the hall.

"Hopefully, Lord Murray is too polite to refuse. It would suit our purpose if Miss Pendleton began to doubt his intentions." Scarlett closed the door and scanned the room. "The furnishings are a little more lavish than those in Lord Craven's powder room, but we should try to piece together what you remember of that night."

"Lord Tregarth has exquisite taste," Cassandra agreed, surveying the sumptuous red velvet chaise and the exquisite gilt mirrors. Four dressing screens painted with vivid woodland scenes, nymphs and cherubs, created separate spaces for those ladies who preferred to be discreet. "And his staff clearly have an awareness of the privacy required when a lady attends to her needs."

"Lord Craven is a lech." Scarlett picked up a padded chair from the far side of the room and headed back towards the door.

"No doubt he gets a thrill from imagining a group of ladies all lifting their skirts together while using the bourdaloues."

"What are you doing with that chair?" Verity asked.

"I shall bar the door to stop people entering." Scarlett nodded towards the concealed cupboard next to the screens. "Perhaps there's something wrong with the pulley. The maid in attendance must have gone down to the servants' quarters to see why they're not sending up clean chamber pots."

The lack of clean porcelain supported Scarlett's theory.

Verity gave a curious frown. "The mention of the maid raises an important question, does it not?" She turned to Cassandra. "There must have been a servant in attendance that night. Do you remember seeing a member of staff in Lord Craven's retiring room?"

Before Cassandra could answer, and before Scarlett had wedged the chair's crest rail underneath the handle, the door opened and three ladies burst into the room, laughing about something they had witnessed in the corridor.

Rosamund, her aunt Miss Felicia Fox and Mrs Partridge all came crashing to a halt. As quick as a wink, the smiles slipped from their faces. Rosamund's cheeks flamed berry-red, and she gulped as she struggled to meet Cassandra's gaze.

"Rosamund. How lovely to see you." Cassandra might have rushed forward and hugged her friend had the lady not worn such a tortured expression.

"Cassandra." The strained word left Rosamund's lips before her aunt gave her a hard nudge.

The elder Miss Fox—a spinster of middling years—grabbed Rosamund by the elbow. "We should return to the ballroom. We shall visit the retiring room when it's a little less crowded."

Without uttering another word, without a backward glance or a mouthed apology from Rosamund, the ladies scurried out into the corridor.

Cassandra stared at the door as she struggled with the sudden onset of tears. She understood the reason for her friend's reticence. An unmarried lady could not be seen conversing with one found practically naked in Hyde Park. Losing her reputation was something Cassandra had come to accept. Losing her friend hurt more than she could possibly explain.

Scarlett slammed the door shut and muttered an unladylike obscenity. Then she used the chair to prevent anyone else turning the handle. "What a better world it would be if everyone learnt to show a little kindness and compassion."

Cassandra drew comfort from Scarlett's wisdom. "I have been in Rosamund's position. I know what it's like to be manipulated by those who profess to know better."

"As do I," Verity added. "I was only allowed to speak to those my mother deemed fit."

Cassandra was the daughter of an equally overbearing parent. "How can I blame Rosamund when it's obvious she's frightened?"

"One could see the warring emotions in her eyes," Verity agreed. "But you must put it from your mind. It was easy for me. No one knew me here in town, and I married Lawrence before there was even a hint of a scandal."

"And I already had a scandalous reputation when I married Damian," Scarlett added. "You have suffered despicably, and we will help you in your fight for justice."

Their kind words roused a weak smile. "You might find it hard to believe after the terrible things I've said, but I care deeply for Benedict."

Scarlett grinned. "You're in love with him. I saw it on your wedding day, and I saw it when you parted just now in the ballroom."

Was it so glaringly obvious?

Indeed, she was so in love with Benedict Cavanagh it hurt.

"I have always loved him," she admitted. "Which is why I must clear his name. I must prove it wasn't Benedict who orchestrated my ruination."

Scarlett clapped her hands. "Then let us get on with the

task. Sit down." Scarlett led her to the chaise and Cassandra dropped into the seat. "Close your eyes. I want you to imagine you're at Lord Craven's ball. Do you remember feeling dizzy?"

"Yes." It took a moment to form a mental picture, but she remembered the confounding noise, the heat, the nausea.

"Do you recall walking along the corridor to the retiring room? There is a landscape painting of a field littered with haystacks to the left of the door. To the right is a marble bust of Emperor Commodus."

A vision of her grabbing the bust as it wobbled on the plinth flashed into her mind. "I think I stumbled in the doorway."

"And did someone come to your aid?"

She shook her head. "No. People thought it amusing." She could almost hear the strains of laughter from those in the vicinity.

"But you found your way into the room?" Verity clarified.

"Yes, I remember the heavy scent of perfume clawing at my throat. Nausea roiled in my stomach." At some point, she had collapsed to the floor. "Someone helped me to a chair. The room spun round and round, and I heaved ready to cast up my accounts."

"Can you recall anything else?" Scarlett asked.

Cassandra screwed her eyes tight, but the images wouldn't come. "No, nothing. Everything went black."

"What about sounds?" Verity said. "They're often overlooked."

A sudden knock on the retiring room door made it difficult to concentrate, but eventually her mind drifted back to that night. Indeed, she recalled the distant echo of voices. Two women. One barking orders. One obeying. "Someone sent the maid to fetch a flask of smelling salts." The scene faded into silence. "I'm sorry. That is all I remember."

"You've done exceptionally well," Scarlett said.

Cassandra forced her eyes open and blinked past the flashing lights blurring her vision. "We're no closer to finding the person responsible than we were a few minutes ago."

Verity arched a neat brow. "On the contrary, the maid is hardly likely to forget the incident, and will remember who sent her for smelling salts."

Scarlett placed a reassuring hand on Cassandra's shoulder. "The question now is, which one of us will visit Lord Craven and ask to question the maids?"

Lord Craven had a way of making the hair on Cassandra's nape prickle to attention. Indeed, she might have added him to the list of suspects had he not been playing cards with her father. "Best we send a man. I shall ask Lord Tregarth to make the enquiries. He hates the thought of people blaming Benedict for what's happened, and he has the strength of character to demand Lord Craven's attention."

Another loud rap on the door made them jump. "Hello?" called a high-pitched voice. "Is anyone in there?" The handle rattled.

"Excellent, now we all have a task to complete," Scarlett said, seemingly ignoring the cries, but then she crossed the room and moved the chair. She opened the door and greeted the two matrons waiting to use the bourdaloues. "There's a problem with the pulley system. The maid asked that we limit the use of the room until they fix the issue."

"I see." The matron looked down her pointed nose. "Someone should inform Tregarth."

Cassandra smiled. "I shall see to the task."

"And we shall return to the ballroom." Scarlett led the way out into the corridor, and they gathered near an alcove. "I will inform Tregarth. You'll want to avoid him seeing your bruise. I dread to think what he will do when he sees the cut on Benedict's cheek."

Lord Tregarth would bring the devil's wrath down upon the man who had deliberately hurt his son. "The sooner we find the culprit, the better."

"Agreed." Verity's gaze drifted past Cassandra's shoulder. "Prepare yourself," she said with an air of caution. "Your friend Miss Atwood is heading this way. I only hope you receive a better reception this time around."

Having spoken to Sybil since losing her good name, Cassandra had every confidence the lady would approach. Indeed, Sybil's green eyes widened as their gazes locked, and she hurried to join them. Introductions were made, though the ladies had spoken briefly on the morning of the wedding.

"I much prefer you in green." Cassandra surveyed Sybil's emerald gown and noted the neckline was cut a little lower than most gowns in her wardrobe. "Black is so unbecoming."

Doubtless sensing Cassandra wanted a moment alone with Sybil, Scarlett and Verity made their apologies and headed back to the ballroom.

Sybil clutched Cassandra's arm and drew her further into the alcove. "I don't suppose Mr Cavanagh knows anything about the auction I mentioned?"

"No, he's heard nothing. But Mr Daventry is here this evening. Perhaps Benedict will have a chance to speak to him." Oh, it felt so good having someone treat her normally and not as if she had two heads.

"Yes, the devil is here with his mistress, Mrs Sinclair. I'm taking note of all the gentlemen he speaks to, but I lost him somewhere in the ballroom and suspect he's ravishing the widow in the garden."

Only rakes out looking for sport did that, but then Mr Daventry *had* devoured a lady's mouth while standing in a bookshop.

"There must be a reason why he won't tell you about the auction." Cassandra was grateful for an opportunity to focus on someone else's problems as opposed to her own. "If he means to be rid of your father's possessions, I cannot see why he wouldn't sell them to you."

"No, and I cannot understand why my father sold the items

to Mr Daventry in the first place. What would a licentious scoundrel want with scientific equipment?"

"Perhaps there is more to Mr Daventry's character than meets the eye." Atticus Atwood had admired intelligence and cared little for a gentleman's lineage. "He must have thought highly of Mr Daventry to sell the rogue his personal possessions."

Sybil snorted. "I have yet to find evidence to support that theory. Mr Daventry is the most obnoxious man ever to make my acquaintance. He is rather blatant in his indifference. Perhaps if I had your golden locks and trim figure, he might be less rude."

"Perhaps Mr Daventry shows the world what he wants them to see—a man with no interest in anything other than seducing women."

Cassandra was full of ideas when it came to assessing Sybil's problem, useless when it came to solving her own.

"I hate to pester you when you have so much to contend with already." Sybil captured Cassandra's hand. "But if Mr Cavanagh could discover any information about the auction, I would be eternally grateful."

"I cannot promise Benedict will have any success, but he said he would speak to Mr Daventry. They have—"

A discreet cough behind forced Cassandra to stop abruptly and glance over her shoulder. Lord Murray stood a mere foot away looking handsome and elegant in a forest-green coat—another recent purchase as she had never seen the garment. Nor had she seen the large ruby pin decorating his cravat.

"Cassandra, forgive the intrusion, but may I have a moment of your time?"

"I would have liked a moment of your time, Timothy, but you preferred to drink port and talk politics." She turned back to Sybil, but the notion that she might press Lord Murray to confess proved too tempting an opportunity to miss. She gripped Sybil's hand. "I shall send word as soon as Benedict discovers the relevant details. I must speak to Lord Murray."

Sybil nodded, but then suspicion clouded her vibrant green eyes. "Promise me you won't venture from this corridor."

Having heard the remark, Lord Murray scoffed. "Cassandra has nothing to fear from me, Miss Atwood. I'm not the rogue who kidnapped her if that is what you're implying."

"You clearly had a motive, my lord," Sybil countered, not the least bit afraid of the peer. "Forgive me for being slightly apprehensive when you seek private counsel."

"Can a man not show concern for the lady he was supposed to marry?"

Sybil lifted her chin. "Not when you gave up the right in deference to your reputation."

Before they drew attention from the gossips hiding in dark corners, Cassandra drew Sybil aside. "I shall speak to Lord Murray near that alcove." She pointed to the place vacated by two whispering women. A place closer to the ballroom. "Would you find Benedict and tell him where I am?" The strains of a waltz reached her ears. "He should be waiting near the terrace doors."

Sybil nodded and lowered her voice. "Despite what Lord Murray says, do not go anywhere with him."

"I won't."

Placated, Sybil cast Lord Murray a disapproving glare before heading back along the corridor towards the ballroom.

Cassandra led Lord Murray towards the empty alcove. "No doubt this won't take long. So, what is it you wish to say?"

Lord Murray stepped closer. Too close. The annoying lock of dark hair fell over his brow as he bent his head. "I put you in a bit of a predicament last night when I spoke about your love for me in front of your husband. It's clear he admires you greatly"—the lord's gaze dropped to the exposed curve of her breasts—"as do I."

Cassandra shrugged. "It is of no consequence."

"Cavanagh rescued something of your reputation, and for that needs commending."

"He certainly does."

"But everyone knows you despise him, and it's only a matter of time before he takes a mistress." Lord Murray moistened his almost absent top lip. "My advice is to approach your marriage with the same mindset as your husband."

Cassandra blinked rapidly, astounded at his audacity. "And what mindset would that be?"

His smirk spelt mischief. "Oh, I think you know. When two people share a deep affection, as we do, it is understandable that we would want to satisfy our curiosity."

Good Lord!

How had she been so blind as to think this man was something other than a repulsive leech? She had every intention of explaining exactly how she felt, but not before trying to gain the truth from the blood-sucking parasite.

"How could I trust you when you're the one who had most to gain from my ruination? Perhaps if you had an alibi, I might have more faith. What time *did* you leave Lord Craven's ball that night?"

Lord Murray arched an arrogant brow and puffed his chest. "Around midnight. Twenty people can verify my claim."

"Name them."

"Name them?" he echoed. "I was three sheets to the wind. Three parts foxed. Ask Craven. Ask his footmen. They assisted numerous guests into the carriages lining the street."

"Surely your mother wasn't sotted. Can she not name those you passed pleasantries with on the way out?"

"My mother?" He was about to say something else but snapped his mouth shut.

"She did accompany you home?"

Distrust flared. Lord Murray always played the doting son. Indeed, he never drank to excess in the matron's company.

"My mother took ill with a megrim and left early. Hencote returned with the carriage to ferry me home."

Cassandra stopped breathing for a moment. She had known

of Lord Purcell's early exit but not that of Lady Murray. Were the two colluding to bring about her downfall?

"Did you see your mother upon your return home?" Suspicion slithered and writhed in her chest. "Can anyone confirm she was ill? Can anyone vouch she was not ruining your prospects of marrying me in the hope you might find someone with a larger dowry?"

Lord Murray jerked his head back, aghast at her blatant accusation. "I know you're upset about the whole affair, but I'll not stand here and listen to you slander my mother."

"Then leave." Cassandra flicked her fingers in a gesture of contempt. "Scuttle back to your mother and pander to her whims."

"What the devil's got into you?"

"I am tired of listening to your pathetic drivel." Honesty proved remarkably refreshing. "You defend your mother because the two of you probably planned the whole thing."

"How many more times must I tell you? I had nothing to do with what happened to you that night. Good God, I'll find witnesses to prove my innocence, and then I shall expect a written apology for the despicable way you've behaved."

Cassandra slapped a hand to her chest. "The way I have behaved?" An incredulous chuckle escaped. "Do you know, I should applaud the person who sought to leave me lying on the wet grass half-naked. Due to their wicked intervention, I am married to a real gentleman, not a blithering idiot who cowers behind the sofa when his mother enters the room."

People were beginning to stare.

Good. She was the scandalous wife of a scandalous son and with it came a responsibility to cause a stir.

"And I find I must refuse your offer of a dalliance. I spoke in earnest when I said I've never loved you." She had liked him, but then she had known little of his true character. Lord Murray hid behind a wall of conceit. Benedict never pretended to be anything other than himself.

She might have stopped there, but her handsome husband appeared in the hallway, his features granite-like, his eyes dangerously wild.

"And just so we are clear," she said through gritted teeth. "There is only one man I have ever loved, and I am fortunate enough to have married him." She pushed past the obnoxious lord and marched towards Benedict.

"Is there a problem?" Anger infused his tone. "Miss Atwood said Lord Murray insisted on speaking to you privately. I can speak to him privately, too, should he become a nuisance." He sharpened his gaze as he stared at the lord. "Though I doubt he will like what I have to say."

"Come. I shall tell you about it on the way home." She wouldn't lie and so didn't want to be in the same vicinity as Lord Murray when her husband learned of the lord's suggestive proposition. "Though I did discover something of interest to our investigation."

"I have information to impart, too, but not here. I cannot continue to avoid my father, and fear what he will do to Murray when he discovers we were attacked outside Mrs Crandall's abode."

"Is it not better he hears it from you than from someone else?"

"I don't need my father to fight my battles. And the only people who know about the attack are Wycliff and Trent."

"And the Murrays, although they're unlikely to spread gossip when it makes them look guilty."

"Agreed. Wycliff will speak to my father and explain our need to visit the Serpentine as part of our investigation. That should appease him until Dermot Flannery discovers who hired the brutes."

Dread played havoc with her insides at the thought of returning to the Serpentine. "Must we go to Hyde Park tonight?" Having no memory of what had occurred during those lost hours before she had woken, her mind had concocted a host of terrible scenarios. "Is it not better to go during daylight hours?"

He slipped a comforting hand around her waist. "No one will harm you, not while you're with me. But if you've any hope of remembering something, it is better to visit at night."

"Then let us leave now." A troubling sense of trepidation took hold. What if the blackguards who'd pounced outside Mrs Crandall's house followed them to Hyde Park? "Have you pistols hidden in the carriage?"

Benedict nodded. "A pair in a walnut case."

"Excellent. We'll arm ourselves with those and take Foston. The man is as skilled as a prizefighter when it comes to using his fists."

CHAPTER FOURTEEN

In a bid to avoid his father, Benedict had darted behind a matron whose headdress consisted of a ridiculous plume of peacock feathers. Indeed, he was somewhat relieved when he finally escaped the ballroom and assisted Cassandra into the carriage.

"Foston seems excited to join us on a prowl through the park tonight." Cassandra relaxed into the seat opposite, her gaze trained on him from the dim confines of the carriage. "I think he enjoys a fight as much as you do."

"It's not the physical aspects of a fight I love." Having been embroiled in a fair few skirmishes, Benedict spoke from experience. "It's the look of shock on my opponent's face when he discovers I hit with the power of a man twice my size."

The carriage jerked forward and picked up speed.

"Well, let's pray our late-night adventure passes without incident." The tremble in her voice conveyed her anxiety. But it was better to face one's fears than avoid them.

"You mean without either of us firing a lead ball at a hired thug."

"Indeed. We have enough to contend with without being hauled to Bow Street to argue a case of self-defence."

"It's not the men from Bow Street who worry me. My father will tear through the *ton* causing untold destruction when the truth comes to light." Tregarth would not sit idle once he'd learned who was responsible for the staged ruination in Hyde Park. And woe betide the man who ordered the attack in Theobolds Road. "I would rather deal with the culprit before my father intervenes."

Cassandra nodded. "I should tell you about my conversation with Lord Murray." She paused, and he suspected that whatever she was about to say would rouse his ire. "Other than the fact he suggested we partake in a dalliance, he—"

"He did what!" Benedict shot forward as she confirmed his suspicion. "Murray propositioned you?"

A blush stained her cheeks. "He said it was only a matter of time before you took a mistress. He suggested I make a similar arrangement myself."

"And he thought to offer his services." God damn! He'd wring Murray's neck if he so much as looked at Cassandra in the wrong way. "Before I curse the man to hell, let me make one thing abundantly clear. I made an oath, a promise I mean to keep. I shall bed you, Cassandra, or I shall bed no one. Do you understand?"

Her breathing came a little quicker, a sure sign she found something arousing in his statement. "And I shall have no other man in my bed but you, Benedict. I couldn't bear the thought of anyone else touching me."

"Good!" he snapped. "Fidelity in marriage is non-negotiable." Though he loved his father, it didn't mean he agreed with the way he lived his life. "You're my wife and I expect loyalty. If I cannot trust you, what hope is there?"

"You can trust me." Water welled in her eyes and she darted across the carriage to sit beside him. "I swear I shall never betray your trust again." She spoke so quickly she could hardly catch her breath. She grabbed his hands, avoiding the cuts on his knuckles. "I swear I shall never give you cause to doubt me."

Guilt surfaced for having spoken in so harsh a tone. "Cassandra, I'm not angry with you. I'm angry with Murray for his blatant audacity. His offer reeks of disrespect and I cannot sit by and let him treat you so abominably." On the morrow, he would visit Murray and make his position clear. Perhaps the lord needed a physical reminder of what Benedict might do if he overstepped the mark.

A tear trickled down Cassandra's cheek. "I wish we could go back to that terrible day five years ago. I wish I'd had the strength to tell my father to go to the devil."

While he appreciated the sentiment, this wasn't a conversation he wished to revisit. "That time has passed. We're different people now." It was difficult to acknowledge, but he was a better man because of his heartbreak. "I doubt I would be as strong."

"Yes." Desire clouded her gaze as she scanned the breadth of his chest. "And you're so strong, Benedict. The strongest man I know. Power radiates from every aspect of your being." She released his hands, caressed the muscles in his upper arms. "I've always wanted you, but never as much as I want you now."

"Now?" Her amorous words brought lustful urges rushing to the fore. "Since we've reunited? Or do you mean to ride me senseless in a moving carriage?"

She gulped a breath. "The latter has immense appeal."

Bloody hell!

The sudden rush of blood to his cock made him light-headed. "Then might I suggest you straddle my thighs and let me drive deep into your willing body."

She needed no further inducement. Indeed, in a sudden flurry of activity that had him yanking down the blinds, she hiked her skirts up to her waist as he fumbled frantically with the buttons on his breeches.

"I would prefer to pleasure you first," he said as she climbed on top of him. "It will be easier for you if you're aroused."

"I'm aroused. Make no mistake. The intense throbbing is driving me insane." She raised her skirts higher, giving him an ample view of milky-white thighs and soft buttocks. "We've a lifetime to focus on pleasure. I just need you to join with me."

An explosion of lust crashed through him. This woman was his fate, his future, his destiny. Perfect for him in every way. He positioned himself at her entrance, gripped her hips and plunged home.

"Christ!" She was so hot, so wet, so eager to sheath his cock.

"Benedict!" The first thrust tore his name from her lips.

Hell, he had conjured this scenario so many times. The reality exceeded every wild fantasy. "God, love, you must have been dying for me to take you." Her muscles hugged his shaft. "Show me how much you want me."

She claimed his lips in a frenzied kiss, a hungry kiss that saw her drive her tongue deep into his mouth looking for a means to feed her craving. He felt the same sense of desperation writhing in his veins. A need to love his wife, fuck his wife, worship every inch of her mind and body. He wanted to devour her, consume her, hold her so damn close, never let her go.

He tore his mouth from hers, rained kisses down the column of her throat, took to sucking and nipping and feasting on the soft curve of her breasts.

"I'm so damn hard for you." He was so bloody ravenous. But his need for her went beyond physical lust. She completed him. His soul ached to have her, ached just as much as his throbbing erection. "Do what you want with me. I have always been yours to command." He was but a slave to her will.

"I've wanted you for so long, Benedict. Show me what to do."

"With pleasure." He cupped her bare buttocks, guided her up and down his shaft until she found her own rhythm. And what a delightful rhythm it was.

Intoxicated, his head fell back against the squab as he watched his wife lose herself in her passions. She rode him with such wanton abandon he was fixated on every facial expression, every moan and pleasurable sigh.

You were always mine.

You were always meant for me.

He pressed his fingers to her intimate place and massaged in teasing strokes, observed every little shudder, every needy plunge in this erotic dance. The urge to confess his love was like a coil winding tighter inside, but he wanted her undivided attention when he made such an important declaration.

She came apart straddled across his thighs, her body convulsing around him, drawing him deeper, pumping his cock. A roar of satisfaction burst from him when he came seconds later.

As he held her close while their breathing settled, his emotions were torn. Torn between wanting to kill the person who had hurt her, and wanting to kneel at their feet to thank them for their wicked intervention.

"That was simply a prelude to what you might expect when we return home," he said, catching his breath. "I intend to worship you slowly, with more care and attention."

"Must we go to Hyde Park?" she asked, her voice dreamy with sated desire.

"While I would like nothing more than to explore our burning attraction, we must work to bring the villain to justice." He retrieved a handkerchief from his coat pocket and handed it to her.

A sweet sigh left her lips when she came up on her knees and he withdrew from her body. "I long for the day when this is over." She crossed the carriage, straightened her skirts and flopped into the seat. "Perhaps we might go to Brighton. I'll never forget the summer we spent there."

"We were in love. Every aspect is ingrained in my memory, too." While he straightened his clothes and fastened the buttons on his breeches, he considered the possibility that their feelings hadn't changed. She certainly loved the intimacy. But did she still love him? "Like you, I trust we will see an end to our problems soon."

Neither spoke for a time.

He raised the blinds and noted their direction. "We shall arrive at our destination in a matter of minutes. I told Foston to park near Hyde Park Corner."

"Why there? Do you suspect the villain carried me to the Serpentine through that gate?"

"As it's impossible to predict which entrance the kidnapper used, I suggest we start at the Serpentine and inspect all possible routes." Benedict retrieved the walnut case from the cupboard beneath his seat. He flicked open the catches and scanned the pistols cushioned in burgundy velvet. "It might surprise you to learn that I've never had cause to use these. Still, it pays to be cautious."

Foston parked the carriage in Brick Lane. Having given him command of both pistols, the coachman accompanied them into the grounds via Hyde Park Corner and followed at a reasonable distance behind.

Cassandra drew her cloak firmly across her chest as they moved past the entrance to the Row and navigated the tree-lined walkway leading down to the Serpentine. The cold night air burned his lungs every time he inhaled, though he suspected his wife's shivering stemmed from fear, not the plummeting temperature.

A sinister energy lingered in the park at night. A strange and stirring atmosphere. The full moon turned the surrounding sky from inky blue to sulphur-grey. An eerie mist clung to the ground, a ghostly blanket swirling about their feet. The trees were but black shadows, sturdy onlookers watching the fools who thought it safe to take a stroll at such an ungodly hour.

"The park is deserted." Cassandra hugged his arm and shivered again as she looked beyond the silvery moonlit path. While the trunks of the trees stood rigid in the wind, the leaves whispered suspicious secrets. "Whoever brought me here has no fear of the dark."

"A man capable of committing such a heinous crime has no

conscience." Which was why Benedict was drawn to the notion that Lord Purcell was the culprit. "A man capable of performing the devil's work is at home in ominous surroundings."

"Sometimes I wonder if I might wake and find this is all a dream."

Her choice of words intrigued him. "A dream, not a dreadful nightmare?"

"It would have been a nightmare had I not married you." Her tone rang of gratitude. Gratitude was not the emotion he wished to rouse.

"Marriage was the only way to salvage the remnants of your reputation," he said, stating the obvious.

"You mistake me. Marrying you has always been my dream. A dream I never imagined would come to fruition."

He had no desire to dredge up old memories, to blame her for being too weak to disobey her father. The intimate moments they'd shared these last two days brought hope for the future, and so the best course of action was to focus on the present moment.

"Then we should both count ourselves fortunate. Marrying has always been my dream, too."

"Mrs Crandall said you'd sworn never to marry."

He cast her a sidelong glance and waited for her to meet his gaze. "I swore I would marry no one but you and I meant it."

They stared at each other for a few heartbeats before she said, "Then we have every reason to celebrate." Her smile brightened her eyes and the need to find the villain who had carried out the pernicious act burned fiercely in his chest. "Indeed, I cannot wait until we can put this matter behind us and work on building a future."

"With the Wycliffs and Trents on the case, the truth will prevail."

She nodded. "Before we left your father's ball you said you had news to impart."

"Yes. Numerous people can attest to the fact that Murray was one of the last to leave Lord Craven's ball. Mrs Beckwith remembers him stumbling down the front steps." She'd used the words *drunken buffoon* three times or more.

"That's because his mother left early after suffering a megrim. He took advantage of her absence to get thoroughly sotted."

A sudden movement in the parkland to their left captured Benedict's attention. He brought Cassandra to an abrupt halt and motioned for Foston to investigate. The coachman moved stealthily from the path and disappeared into the darkness.

"Should we let him go alone?" Cassandra whispered, her breathless pants creating puffs of white mist against the cold night air.

"He's armed, and most likely it's just lovers looking for somewhere to satisfy their urges." Still, Benedict's heart raced until Foston returned to resume his position, a curt nod being the man's only indication it was safe to proceed.

"Perhaps this is a foolish idea." Cassandra gripped Benedict's arm as he urged her forward. "The thought that the cruel devil left me here alone at night chills me to the bone."

Benedict had to agree. The dark expanse played havoc with one's imagination. It wasn't hard to envisage evil rogues hiding in the blackness, waiting to commit vile deeds.

"We'll walk as far as the Serpentine." He did not want to cause her undue distress. Perhaps she was right. It would be better to inspect the park during the day. "We'll visit the spot where I found you and then return to the carriage."

"Very well." After a brief pause while drawing in a deep breath, she said, "Let us continue our conversation about Lord Murray while we walk. It will help to occupy my mind."

While Benedict attempted to recall what he had told her thus far, another thought occurred to him. "Did you say Lady Murray left the ball early?"

"Yes, apparently she took ill with a megrim."

"Does that not seem suspicious to you?" It gave Lady

Murray opportunity. As for motive, well, perhaps she wanted her son to marry a lady whose father wasn't so domineering.

"It does, but then someone of Lady Murray's size could not have carried me from the gate to the Serpentine."

"No." It was a fair walk without the burden of lugging a body. A treacherous walk in the dark. "Then she had an accomplice."

"It has to be Lord Purcell. Did you get the chance to question him tonight?"

Benedict had searched every room, had scoured the house looking for the arrogant lord, but to no avail. "Purcell neglected to attend. I would have asked Tregarth but didn't want him to see the cut on my face."

Cassandra gave a curious hum. "That surprises me. Like my father, Lord Purcell takes every opportunity to impress his lofty opinions."

"Having insulted my father, no doubt Purcell sought to avoid a confrontation."

"Or he is guilty of the crime and is keen to avoid drawing undue attention."

Thinking about motives and identifying the real culprit hurt Benedict's brain. They had to find evidence—legitimate proof of guilt—not base their opinions on supposition. Either that, or they had to press the suspects for a confession. Things might become clearer once Trent had questioned the groom and Dermot Flannery had spoken to Finnigan.

As they moved closer to the Serpentine, Cassandra stopped abruptly. "There's something near that tree. A strange shadow. No, a man."

She had focused her attention on the vagabond sitting on the ground, leaning against a tree trunk. The man was buried beneath a mound of moth-eaten coats, his eyes hidden by the brim of his dusty hat. The tip of his long, unkempt beard touched his chest, and he appeared to be sleeping.

The terrier sprawled at his side jumped to its feet as they

approached. The snappy creature barked—a high-pitched and highly irritating noise—as it had done on the night Benedict came to the park to avoid sleeping with his wife.

Cassandra tugged Benedict's arm as she shuffled backwards in terror. But the dog was all bark, no bite.

"The animal is trained to protect its master's belongings." Benedict gestured to the cloth sack on the ground, which made the dog snarl and snap all the more.

Cassandra winced at the sound. "That bark …" She shook her head and screwed her eyes shut. "It seems familiar."

The vagabond raised the brim of his hat and scanned the quality of their clothing. He drew the dog to heel and then they both settled back to resume their light slumber.

"Do you remember the dog barking on the night you were kidnapped?" If she could remember that, then other memories might return.

"Yes." Confusion marred her brow. "Though it was not long afterwards that I woke to a dawn mist."

"What are you saying?" Benedict engaged his logical brain. "That the perpetrator carried you to the Serpentine while you were waking from your drug-induced state? That he had not left you alone in the park all night?"

Cassandra shrugged. "I'm not sure. My memory is so hazy."

It had always struck him as odd that a man would play hazard with a woman's life when the intention was simply to ruin her reputation. A vulnerable woman left alone for hours was a target for those disreputable men who prowled the park. So the villain had kept Cassandra safe until the appointed time. The time when Benedict arrived to play his part.

"Perhaps this fellow might shed some light on the event." With Cassandra still clinging to his arm, Benedict approached the vagabond. He coughed and cleared his throat. "Forgive me for disturbing your rest, but I am looking for a witness to a tragic event that occurred here almost a week ago."

The terrier barked though the sound lacked conviction.

"Sir," Benedict continued. "Someone abducted my wife and left her near the Serpentine. We are trying desperately to find the fiend responsible. You might help by permitting us to ask a few questions."

The man did not stir.

"Please, sir," Cassandra implored. "I cannot rest until I find the felon." The dog cocked its head, looked at her and then at the lifeless figure propped against the tree. "I beg you, sir, help me."

A second or two later, the vagabond raised his head. He pushed his hat up past his weather-beaten forehead and studied her intently. "Not someone, a man," he said in a croaky Northern accent, a voice unused to conversation.

"I beg your pardon?"

"A man carried you to the lake."

Benedict's heart pounded although the vagabond hadn't told them anything they didn't already know. "Do you know what time it was?"

The vagabond mumbled. "Happen I misplaced my gold pocket watch, but it was just before sunrise."

Benedict turned to Cassandra. "So the devil kept you prisoner before bringing you here."

"I suppose it was the most logical thing to do under the circumstances." She stepped forward and crouched beside the fellow. "Can you recall anything else? A description of the gentleman, perhaps?" She spoke quickly, with a desperation Benedict shared. "Was he a young man with dark hair and pristine clothes?"

She meant was it Lord Murray.

"It's hard to say." The fellow drew a dirty hand down his scruffy beard. "He was tall, was fancy-like, had a face of stone. He carried you down to the lake and I never saw him again."

No, because Benedict had arrived via Hyde Park Corner mere minutes later.

Cassandra straightened and tightened her cloak across her

chest. "It must have been apparent that something nefarious was afoot. Did you not think to alert the watchman?"

"And have the nabob say I robbed him. He goes home and I'm charged with being a liar and a thief." The man reached out and stroked his dog. "So no, I didn't think to alert the watchman."

A tense silence descended.

Cassandra's mood turned subdued.

Benedict drew a coin from his pocket and was about to hand it to the vagabond when the fellow said, "I don't accept charity, but give it to Frankie. He's a scavenger and will take anything he finds."

Despite the odd request, Benedict placed the coin near the dog's front paws. The animal took the coin in its mouth and dropped it into its master's outstretched hand.

"We should leave now," Cassandra said, steering Benedict away from the fellow sneaking the coin into his ragged coat pocket. "I'm cold to my bones, tired and just want to go home."

Benedict drew her into an embrace and rubbed her upper arms in comforting strokes. "This will all be over soon. I promise."

She placed her head on his shoulder, wrapped her arms around his waist. "A part of me fears what will happen when we learn the truth." She looked up at him, her blue eyes pleading. "Promise me nothing will change between us. Promise me that what we've rekindled will only go from strength to strength."

Had someone predicted he would marry Cassandra Mills, that she would embrace him, give him hope for the future, he would have thrown them in shackles and carted them off to Bedlam.

Sliding the wedding band onto her finger had helped to awaken the old feelings trapped inside. Every time he closed his mouth over hers, every time she hugged him tight as he buried himself deep inside her body, he felt the bitterness and distrust melt away.

She was the love of his life.

Of that, he was certain.

"I promise," he said.

While he had breath in his body, nothing would come between them again.

CHAPTER FIFTEEN

A series of light knocks on the bedchamber door roused Cassandra from her slumber. "Madam, are you awake?" Lucy, her new lady's maid—as the earl refused to let her previous maid leave his employ—spoke with some urgency. "Madam?"

"Just a moment." Cassandra tried to move, but Benedict's muscular arm and thigh held her pinned to the bed. Not that she had any complaint.

Lifting the sheets, she studied her husband's firm buttocks as he lay sprawled on his front. Blessed Mary! They had made love until the first light of dawn, and still, she wanted to devour every impressive inch. Perhaps once she had dealt with Lucy, she might tease her husband awake.

After raising his arm gently and shuffling out of bed, she threw on her wrapper and padded to the door. "Is everything all right?" Cassandra slipped out onto the landing so as not to disturb Benedict.

"You've a visitor, ma'am. Mr Wycliff is here and wishes to speak to you and Mr Cavanagh as soon as you're able."

"Mr Wycliff? Oh!" That put paid to all notions of an intimate morning spent frolicking in bed. But Damian Wycliff would not make an early morning call unless it was important. "What time is it?"

"A little after ten, ma'am." Lucy's cheeks flushed. "Mr Wycliff said he'll join you for breakfast, that you must eat before you go tearing off to cause mischief and mayhem."

Mischief and mayhem?

Good Lord!

He must have learned something vital to their investigation.

"Have Mrs Rampling serve breakfast in the dining room." She had hoped to have a tray sent up to their bedchamber. "And set a place for Mr Wycliff."

Lucy glanced briefly at her shoes. "Mr Wycliff accosted Mrs Rampling and has already made the arrangements. He's a very persuasive gentleman, ma'am. Indeed, he's taken his seat at the table and has almost emptied the coffee pot." The maid looked apologetic when she added, "I have been knocking for some time."

"Then kindly tell Mr Wycliff that we will be with him shortly."

Lucy's mouth opened and closed so many times she resembled a fish plucked from the water. "He … well …"

"What else did Mr Wycliff say?" Cassandra knew enough about Damian Wycliff to know he took pleasure from being facetious.

"Mrs Rampling said I'm to tell you that Mr Wycliff has taken command of the broadsheets. He said that he's happy to wait as not all appetites are satisfied around the dining table."

Heat rose to Cassandra's cheeks. The urge to tease the scandalous gentleman took hold. "Tell Mr Wycliff that we will be with him shortly unless something unexpected arises in which case we shall be thirty minutes."

Lucy dipped a curtsy and went to relay the message.

Something important had arisen. After receiving tuition in the art of pleasuring her husband, she brought him to a thrilling climax in a matter of minutes.

"Wycliff must have news of our attackers else he would never call at this hour." Benedict dressed quickly in the crumpled garments strewn across the bedchamber floor. The clothes she had practically ripped from his muscular body last night.

She chose a pale pink morning dress from the armoire and Benedict helped to fasten her stays—taking advantage of the opportunity to stroke and caress her breasts. His attentions distracted from the sudden flurry of nerves fluttering in her throat.

They entered the dining room to find Mr Wycliff relaxing in a chair, reading the broadsheets and sipping coffee. It was evident he hadn't been home since leaving Lord Tregarth's ball. He wore the same coat and cravat. His sculpted jaw bore the dark shadow of stubble, and the pinky whites of his eyes suggested a distinct lack of sleep. Hence his need to drink copious amounts of coffee.

"Ah." Mr Wycliff came to his feet and bowed to her. With a mischievous grin, he scanned Benedict's rumpled attire. "I see I'm not the only one surviving on limited sleep." Having taken position at the head of the table, he glanced at the other seats. "Would you prefer I move?"

"Sit where you feel most comfortable," Benedict said. He waited for the footman to draw out her chair before sitting opposite, to the right of Mr Wycliff. "I trust you're here because you have news from Dermot Flannery."

Mr Wycliff flicked his coattails and sat down, his amused expression fading. "Eat, and then I shall begin by telling you what happened when I left Tregarth's ball last night." He gestured to the covered silver platters on the sideboard. "You both look as though you need a hearty breakfast."

After their rampant activities, she was famished. But how could she eat when her stomach roiled with anxiety? "I shall have coffee and toast," she said and set about helping herself from the rack. The footman stepped forward and poured her beverage.

Benedict filled his plate with ham and poached eggs. "I'm so ravenous I could pick the meat off a carcass."

Mr Wycliff glanced at them through teasing eyes. "There are a few activities that bring about a sudden need for sustenance." He seemed in no rush to inform them of the night's events. "Walking by the sea is one."

"Please. Do not keep us in suspense any longer," Cassandra said, swallowing a sip of coffee. "My heart is likely to give out if you do not begin your story soon."

"Forgive me. As the bearer of bad news, there is no way to make this easier for you." Mr Wycliff sighed. "I visited The Silver Serpent after taking Scarlett home. Flannery had information regarding the brute who attacked you in Theobolds Road. Finnigan *is* the name of the man who brandished the blade."

Cassandra straightened. "Then it shouldn't be too difficult to find out who hired him."

Mr Wycliff frowned. "It wasn't. Hence the reason I am here."

"Oh, yes!" She was so tired she could barely think straight. "Of course. Please continue."

"Flannery gathered a few men, and we went in search of Finnigan. We discovered he lives on Skinner Street, off Bishopsgate, found him in a local brothel with his trousers around his ankles and his … well … I'm sure you'd rather I spare you the vision." Mr Wycliff snorted. "How the man attended to the task when he could barely see out of his swollen eyes is anyone's guess."

Benedict paused while cutting into a slice of ham. Despite Mr Wycliff's amusing comment, he did not raise a smile. "Did Finnigan confirm it was Murray who hired him?"

Mr Wycliff's gaze softened when he switched his attention to her. That's when her heart sank to her stomach. A sudden pang warned her to expect the worst.

"A man named Mr Brydden hired them to give you a severe beating."

"Brydden?" Benedict frowned as he met Cassandra's gaze across the table. "Do you know anyone by that name?"

Mr Wycliff watched her intently, as did her husband. An icy chill ran the length of her spine. It penetrated her clothes, seeped into her bones. A cavernous hole opened in her chest. If only it would swallow her up so she wouldn't have to deal with the violent wave of anger about to erupt.

She swallowed past the pain in her throat. Good Lord! The thought of saying the words made her want to retch. "Mr Brydden—" She paused. "Mr Brydden works for my father's man of business." The china cup rattled on the saucer as she gripped the handle. "I'm sure you know what that means."

A deathly silence descended.

No one spoke.

No one moved.

No one breathed.

And then, with a face as thunderous as any god of war, Benedict threw his cutlery onto the plate. He pushed out of the chair and rounded the table.

She was out of her chair in seconds, grabbing his arm. "What are you going to do?"

"What I should have done a long time ago." He yanked his arm free from her grasp.

Mr Wycliff was on his feet, too. "Rash decisions lead to acts of sheer folly. Wait. Take a moment to calm your temper before you do something you may regret."

They chased after Benedict, who was already in the hall, instructing the butler to summon the carriage. "Never mind, Slocombe, I'll walk."

Mr Wycliff continued to offer words of caution, but Benedict wrenched open the front door and took to the street.

"Damnation!" Mr Wycliff shook his head. "I would follow him, but nothing I say will stop his quest for vengeance. For five years, he's let his bitterness for your father fester. I fear it's too late to make him see sense now."

Tears welled in Cassandra's eyes. "I would chase after him, too, but my efforts to make him see sense will fall on deaf ears. I cannot help but feel this is all my fault."

Mr Wycliff touched her gently on the arm. "I'll not lie to you. I have despised you for five years and cannot fathom what the hell you were thinking when you refused his suit. But I believe you love him. And by God, the man is besotted with you."

In a state of panic, she grabbed Mr Wycliff's arm. "I made a dreadful mistake, but we have a real chance of happiness now. Help me. Oh, please help me, Mr Wycliff. Tell me what to do."

Mr Wycliff dragged his hand down his face and sighed. "We must go to Tregarth. He's the only one who has the remotest chance of stopping him doing something foolish. Come. It will take Benedict thirty minutes to reach Cavendish Square on foot. Let's hope his temper has calmed by then. My carriage is waiting outside. Fetch a jacket, and we'll be on our way."

Anger boiled in Benedict's veins. Hot. Molten. Deadly. When he unleashed his rage, he was guaranteed to cause destruction, untold devastation. For years, he had stood aside while Worthen manipulated events to suit his purpose. He had allowed the earl to browbeat Cassandra into refusing his suit. Though he had pushed the thoughts from his mind, he had always felt less of a man for not supporting her, for not pleading, not fighting.

But he was an outcast—a man who anticipated rejection.

The moment Cassandra told him she didn't want him, that he wasn't good enough, was the moment he locked his heart away in a sealed box never to be opened again.

And yet …

Fate had intervened to give them a second chance. A second chance at happiness, a second chance at love. And by all that was holy, he would not let the earl ruin their lives again.

On the march up to Piccadilly, people darted out of his way. No one wanted to approach the crazed gentleman who had taken to cursing and muttering his objections aloud.

The walk up to New Bond Street roused memories of Murray's arrogant grin as he gripped the reins of his new curricle while playing court to Miss Pendleton. Murray might be innocent of hiring a pack of brutish thugs, but he must have had a hand in the game.

Just thinking of Murray kept his fury flaming.

When he eventually reached Worthen's house in Cavendish Square, he hammered the front door so hard he hoped to take the damn thing off its hinges.

"Where the bloody hell is he?" Benedict roared, pushing past the shocked butler and charging into the earl's study.

Worthen shot up from the chair behind the desk, outrage taking command of his countenance. "What's the meaning of this?" He puffed out his chest. "You're the only man who would charge into a peer's house like a raving heathen."

"Heathen!" Benedict marched across the room. "You have the nerve to call me a heathen when you're the one who hired men to kill me. To kill your daughter's husband. Have you not hurt Cassandra enough?"

Benedict remained on the opposite side of the desk, else he was liable to beat the devil, and he was a better man, a more honourable man than that. No. He would end this conversation by naming Tregarth as his second. He would end this bitter feud by frightening this bastard half to death.

"Don't tell me how to deal with my own damn daughter."

Blind fury saw Benedict thump the desk. "You can no longer stake your claim." Neither could he. He did not belong to the group of men who enjoyed dominating their wives. "As my wife, Cassandra falls under my protection. From now on, every pain you inflict on her I shall return tenfold."

He might have used what he knew about the clerk to blackmail the lord, but in any game one held on to their ace card.

"I have proof Mr Brydden hired the thugs to kill me," Benedict continued. "Mr Brydden obeyed the order given by your man of business, who in turn obeyed the order given by you."

"Proof?" the earl scoffed. "Where is your proof?"

"I have a written confession from the man who carried out the attack." He could lie and manipulate men, too, when necessary. "A confession given in front of witnesses."

"What? More heathens from the demimonde? Their word pales next to mine."

Benedict was prepared to tell another lie if it meant wiping the smirk off the lord's face. "Wycliff and his father, the Marquis of Blackbeck, bore witness to the confession. As did the owner of The Silver Serpent. You'll be surprised what some lords will say in exchange for the return of their vowels."

The earl's arrogant expression faltered. He shuffled uncomfortably. "Whatever this miscreant said is a lie. What have I possibly got to gain from making such an arrangement?"

Oh, he had everything to gain—control of his daughter being the primary goal. "If I'm dead, your daughter can marry someone more suitable. As a widow, older men might overlook the scandal created to cause you shame. Somehow you would turn the situation to your advantage."

The earl snorted.

"See, you cannot deny it. Your duplicity is written all over your miserable face. So, as we're the only ones here, and there are no witnesses, why don't you show the courage of your conviction and tell the damn truth?"

A tense silence ensued.

"No? Can you not stand by your decision?" Benedict braced his knuckles on the desk and leaned forward. "Cowards hide behind webs of deceit. Cowards know only dishonesty."

An arrogant smirk played on the earl's thin lips. "Very well." He dropped into the chair. "So I did hire those men, hired them to beat you, not kill you. Though I must admit, the thought of being rid of you has merit."

How Benedict stopped himself from lunging across the desk was anyone's guess. "So you thought a thrashing would keep me in my place?"

"It had nothing to do with you and everything to do with that bloody pompous lord who was supposed to marry my daughter."

"Murray?" It took a few seconds for recognition to dawn. "Ah, you knew that I would eventually find the men responsible and they would reveal that Murray ordered the attack."

"The Murrays cannot treat me this way. They will pay for what they've done. Mark my words."

Benedict exhaled an incredulous snort. "Treat *you* this way? It's your daughter who has suffered. She has suffered your prolonged cruelty her entire life."

He recalled the way Cassandra behaved with quiet timidity in her father's presence. During those times when she had escaped the house to meet him secretly, she was a different person, full of life and vitality.

"In seeking retribution for the Murrays' disrespect, I am seeking retribution for Cassandra's mistreatment," the earl countered.

"Ballocks! You don't give a damn about her. All you care about is what she can give you, what she can bring to the negotiating table." If he closed his eyes, he could still see her struggling on the ground with her attacker, could still hear the thug delivering a hard slap. "When you hired these men, did you know one would assault your daughter?" Benedict thundered. "Did you know she would have to walk amongst her peers with a bruise marring her cheek?"

The earl's chin dropped. "What … I …"

"No, you never think about anything but your own ambitions. I hold you responsible for what happened to her in the park. You may not have kidnapped her from the ball, but by insisting she marry Murray, you arranged her fall from grace."

The sudden slam of the front door, the sound of raised voices and the heavy clip of footsteps in the hall preceded the arrival of Wycliff, Cassandra and Tregarth.

Tregarth wore a navy silk robe and clearly nothing underneath as one could see the dusting of golden hair between the soft lapels. The lord marched around the desk without uttering a word, grabbed Worthen by his cravat and shook him violently.

"You dare threaten the life of my son." Tregarth's face burned red with rage. "I've tolerated your disrespect for long enough. You will meet me at dawn tomorrow in Pickering Place. We will forgo the time granted to cool heads. Name your second. And I shall have mine deliver a formal challenge. Refuse, and I shall denounce you in every broadsheet willing to publish the notice."

Worthen's face blanched as he gulped for breath.

Benedict slammed his hand on the desk. "This is my battle, not yours."

"I have made it mine, and I shall see this matter through to the bitter end." Tregarth tightened his grip on Worthen's cravat. "Name your second."

"I don't need a second," the earl croaked.

"That's because you cannot name a man willing to stand by your side."

"Name yours," Worthen countered.

Tregarth released the lord and grinned. "I'm a man who refuses to bow to convention. A man who would challenge the very foundations of our dignified code. And so I name my daughter-in-law as my second. I name Cassandra Cavanagh."

CHAPTER SIXTEEN

"Would you care to explain what the devil is going on?" Benedict gripped the overhead strap as Mr Wycliff's carriage navigated the busy Mayfair streets. "Have you taken leave of your senses? This has to be the most ridiculous plan I have ever heard. Indeed, were I not so bloody angry, I might find it amusing."

Cassandra disagreed.

She found Lord Tregarth's plan rather ingenious.

Yes, the decision had been made in haste. Yes, it was unheard of for a woman to involve herself in a gentleman's private affair. But Tregarth wanted to teach the earl a lesson. A lesson he would never forget. Her father would never negotiate with her, would refuse to provide a written apology, and so would have to accept the challenge. With his daughter attending the duel, he couldn't use manipulative tricks to sway things to his advantage.

"Well?" Benedict stared at his father. "I should call you out for using my wife so disgracefully."

"It was partly my idea," she interjected, casting her husband a sidelong glance. "In the hope that with me as a witness, my father will behave in a dignified manner." She had prayed they would arrive before Benedict offered his own challenge. The earl would have manipulated the proceedings, found an excuse to fire a lead ball through Benedict's heart.

"Dignified?" Benedict scoffed. When he turned to face her, she saw fear not anger flashing in his handsome blue eyes. "The man sent brutes to attack me, knowing we were together. Worthen cares about no one but himself, has no regard for your safety."

Lord Tregarth muttered a curse. "In his twisted bitterness, the man is determined to ruin your lives. I cannot let that happen." He settled the blanket across his lap. The lord had been so desperate to reach his son before he did something foolish, he'd left the house wearing nothing but an expensive silk robe and Turkish slippers.

"You would have called Worthen out had your father not done so," Mr Wycliff said from the seat opposite. "This way, the matter will be brought to a swift conclusion without loss of life."

"So you sanctioned this foolhardy plan, too?"

Mr Wycliff leaned back against the squab and shrugged. "Under the circumstances, I saw little alternative."

Benedict gave a mocking snort. "And how would you react if your father used Scarlett to prove a point? How would you react if your father snatched away an opportunity to prove your worth?"

Before Mr Wycliff could respond, Lord Tregarth sat forward. "Benedict, I swear that no harm shall come to your wife. I named Cassandra my second because I wanted to show Worthen that she is allied to our family now. As such, she falls under our protection. It's not about proving a point, but about doing everything possible to ensure you live a long and happy life."

"You doubt my skill with a pistol?"

"It is because I know you're a better shot than Worthen that I left my damn house without dressing. He would force you to act dishonourably. He would goad you, torment you with cruel words until you pulled the trigger and had no option but to hop on the next boat leaving Dover."

"I am not without self-control."

"No, but you have reached the end of your tether when it comes to Worthen's disdain. As for me stealing an opportunity to prove your worth, I bear the responsibility for the way you've been treated."

"You're not to blame for Worthen's actions," Benedict said.

"The man sees you as inferior. Am I not to blame for that? I should have considered how my selfish decisions might affect a child born out of wedlock."

Mr Wycliff turned to stare out of the window. Clearly something Lord Tregarth said had touched a nerve.

"Benedict, there's no need to worry about me." She reached for her husband's hand, mindful of the raw skin marring his knuckles. "Your father chose Pickering Place for a reason."

Indeed, the earl had given her a brief education in what wicked things occurred in the smallest square in London. Many men settled their grievances in the secluded courtyard accessed by a narrow passageway.

"I know the owner of The Diamond Club," Lord Tregarth said. Pickering Place was also the home of a notorious gaming hell. "When the battle commences, you will be out of harm's way. You will have the advantage of watching from an upper window of the exclusive club."

A sudden flurry of nerves made Cassandra ask, "And you promise you will only frighten my father into behaving as he should? You won't shoot him?" She despised her father but wouldn't stoop to his barbarous level.

Tregarth pushed a hand through his mop of golden hair. Deep lines formed on his brow. "I shan't hurt him, but I cannot stand idly by and watch him punish my son. Besides, I intend to ignore the rules. I shall pressure him to choose swords. With swords, there can be no accusation of tampering. No sudden shocks."

Benedict exhaled a weary sigh. "Do what you must to satisfy

your need for revenge. After the event, when your efforts fall on deaf ears, I shall approach the matter from another angle. One I imagine will prove a damn sight more effective."

"You've hardly spoken a dozen words since we woke." Cassandra stood next to Benedict as they looked out onto Pickering Place from the large sash window of The Diamond Club. One could not be accused of supporting a duel when one observed proceedings from a bedchamber. "Indeed, other than during intimate relations last night, you've hardly spoken at all."

Benedict slipped his hand around her waist, though his gaze remained focused on the two lords standing in the small courtyard in their shirt sleeves. Both men glared at each other while her father's coachman inspected the swords cushioned in the mahogany case.

"The irony is that the man who defends me is the one whose actions remind me of my illegitimacy. Tregarth wishes to punish Worthen for his conduct because, as gentlemen, they are equally matched. I fall hopelessly short."

"After the dreadful misfortune he's suffered in his life, Tregarth's biggest fear is that you will die, too. He told me he lives to protect you. He means no slight."

"No," Benedict mused as the men took to practising their lunges in the gloomy courtyard. "But I would have preferred to deal with the matter personally."

"I'm sure the future will hold many opportunities to punish my father." The earl deserved Benedict's wrath for arranging the attack, but was living a happy life not the best means of revenge?

"Tregarth is an exceptional swordsman, one of the best. But Worthen knows my father won't kill him."

"Perhaps the duel is a means to satisfy your father's guilt, too."

Benedict snorted as he raised the sash to witness the proceedings. "Who knows what motivates men to act like fools?"

"In your father's case, love is his main motivation." Her father's reason for attending stemmed from a fear of being branded a coward. "My father has no excuse and has been a fool most of his life."

"Still, it must hurt to see him brought to this. You must feel torn between two families."

She considered his remark before turning to face him. "When I said I'm dead inside, I meant it. I'm dead when it comes to caring about my father. Dead to the hundred and one ways he tries to torment me. And I shall never forgive him for the ice-cold fear that encompassed my heart when you battled with those wretched thugs."

Benedict cupped her cheek. "You might be numb to your father's antics, but when it comes to expressing passionate emotions, you're very much alive."

Oh, the merest touch of his fingers sent sparks of energy racing to every nerve. "I could say that you have reawakened something in me, but that would be a lie." Love—wild and untamed—burned brightly in her chest. "Benedict, it would be a lie because I have never stopped loving you, not for a single second. I wish I'd fought for us. If only I'd dared to break free from my father's clutches. To love you as you deserved."

His Adam's apple bobbed rapidly in his throat. *Cassandra* was the only word to leave his lips before Tregarth called out and interrupted the intimate moment.

"What shall it be, Cassandra?" Tregarth braced a hand on his hip. "Will we fight for first blood? Will we fight until one of us can no longer stand, or until one of us draws our last breath?"

Her father's face paled.

Tregarth knew the answer but was determined to milk this event for all it was worth. "Well?" he goaded. "Shall we grant Worthen the same consideration he gave my son?"

"Fight for first blood," she called before Tregarth got carried away and turned settling a debt of honour into a comedic act one witnessed at Vauxhall. "A nick will deem the matter satisfied."

Both men resumed a stable stance and stood some feet apart. Both men kept their keen gazes focused. Alert.

"Am I not granted one final opportunity to make an apology?" her father mocked.

"Your offence negates any request for clemency." Tregarth swiped the air with his blade. "Did you give my son the same consideration when four men decided to teach him a lesson? A lesson that saw him used to exact your revenge on Lord Murray?" He lunged forward.

Her father sidestepped just in time. "Your son ruined my daughter!" he growled through gritted teeth. "Does he not deserve to pay for that?"

Tregarth laughed as he straightened. With an arrogant grin, he stared at his opponent, looking for an opportune moment to strike. "We both know my son is innocent of the crime. When a man loves a woman, he does not abuse her in the worst possible way."

"Cassandra would never have married beneath her station. Why the devil do you think she refused him in the first place?" Her father lashed out, throwing his weight into an attack that lacked finesse.

Tregarth twirled out of harm's way—a confident pirouette. He pointed the tip of his blade at her father. "She refused him because you made it impossible for her to accept."

"Not impossible," Benedict muttered, bracing his hands on the window ledge. "We might have eloped."

Guilt, and a pain she feared would remain constant until the day she drew her last breath, sought to plague her mind, torture her soul. "Benedict, you're the one who professes to not dwell on the past, yet you choose to remind me of my mistake."

"I'm not reminding you of anything," he said, focusing his attention on the sword fight. "I am merely stating that your father is right, mine is wrong. You wouldn't have married me had Murray stepped up to the mark."

The sound of clashing metal in the courtyard echoed her internal conflict. Regret was something she lived with daily. She battled with the turmoil of knowing she was to blame for five years of misery. But she had made an apology. Professed her love. And so refused to dwell on the past any longer.

"You're entitled to your opinion. Having been the one persecuted to the point of madness, I happen to side with your father in this instance." She stared out of the window, too, watching two men consumed with rage act like children. "But you're right. I would have married Lord Murray had a villain not opened my eyes. I would have been lonely and miserable, forever mourning a lost love." She straightened and stepped back from the window. "It might be difficult for you to believe, but I have always loved you. To the depths of my soul. But I am tired of playing the victim. Tired of being the monster who ruined your life. Sick to the stomach of being the obedient daughter hoping for evidence of her parent's love."

She turned and marched towards the bedchamber door.

"Where are you going? You'll prove too much of a distraction if you stand in the courtyard. Your father will use you to gain an advantage."

Weary of the whole damned affair, she left the room and descended the stairs as if her ghosts were snatching at her heels. The hall was deserted. Those men who had slept off their night of drunken tomfoolery had their noses pressed to the windowpanes, too, while placing bets on the bout.

"The sword is an extension of oneself," Lord Tregarth said as he attacked her father with skill and precision. "Every blow I deliver comes from the heart."

Her father was not as fit as Tregarth, nowhere near as agile on his feet. It didn't help that the thick morning mist shrouded the men's legs up to their knees, so one had no hope of gauging a man's movements from his footwork.

Tregarth attacked again in a sequence of moves set to trick one's opponent into making a mistake. Her father struggled against the force of the offensive. He slipped on the flagstones, managed to remain standing, but Tregarth delivered a well-timed swipe to the face.

"Aargh!" Her father's cry rent the air. He dropped his sword, and it clattered on the flagstones. A thin red line marred his cheek. Drops of blood trickled from the wound.

Tregarth straightened. "That is for the cut my son bears on his cheek. From now on, every vile thing you do to him, I shall visit on you tenfold." The lord lowered his sword and stepped back.

She couldn't bear to witness her father's shame and disgrace and so raised the hood on her cloak and hurried along the narrow passageway leading to St James' Street.

It was a five-minute walk to Jermyn Street, but the need to escape came upon her, and so she took to her feet and fled. The sound of booted steps pounding the pavement sent her heart shooting up to her throat.

"Cassandra! Wait!" Benedict called, but she couldn't bring herself to stop running. "Cassandra!"

She ran until her lungs burned, until she could barely catch her breath, until her husband closed the gap between them and grabbed her arm.

Benedict whipped her around to face him. "Did you not hear me call out to you?"

"I—I heard you." She heaved and tried to calm her frantic heart. Tears sprang from nowhere. Not like the tiny droplets heralding the first sign of rain. Huge drops. Huge drops that turned to streaming rivulets running down her cold cheeks.

Benedict drew her into his arms and held her close. "Forgive me. I never meant to cause you distress. I'm a hypocrite who cannot follow his own blasted advice."

She sobbed, sobbed almost as hard as she did the day she thought she'd lost Benedict forever. But the pain in her chest was nowhere near as intense. Nothing would ever match the heart-wrenching agony she'd experienced that day.

"You spoke the truth," she mumbled somewhere into his cravat. "And I would rather hear your honest opinion than hear lies."

"The ridiculous thing is I no longer care what happened in the past." Muscular arms enveloped her in a warm cocoon. "For years, I continued our bitter war with words when I could have defused the situation, helped to calm our ragged emotions."

Cassandra looked up at him. "Every harsh word I spoke came from the pain of losing you. I only agreed to marry Lord Murray because I hoped to escape my father's clutches." Even then, she was preoccupied with trying to please the heartless earl. "But I could never have loved Murray, not the way I love you."

He brushed away the tendrils of hair stuck to her wet cheeks. "I know. I feel the depth of your love in every kiss. When I enter your body, you hold me as if you never want to let go."

"I never want to be without you again. All this trauma, all these lies and secrets, I'm frightened of what they will reveal. I'm scared our parents' hatred will drive a wedge between us. God, Benedict, I'm terrified of waking up one morning to find this has all been a twisted dream, a cruel nightmare. To find you still despise me, still blame me for ruining everything."

He cupped her cheeks, wiped away her tears with the pads of his thumbs. "Never, not when you rejected my suit, not when you hurled your abuse, did I despise you." He bent his head and kissed her mouth. "I have loved you from the first moment we met. Nothing will temper the love burning in my chest. I love you more now than I ever have. Let us return home, let me spend the rest of the day showing you just how much."

A joyous euphoria flooded her body. "You still love me?" The sudden surge of emotion left her unsteady on her feet.

A smile touched his delectable lips. "I'm so in love with you I have to stop myself from dancing in the street."

She swallowed down tears of happiness. "We never had a chance to waltz at your father's ball. Perhaps you might like to dance with me now."

Benedict scanned their surroundings. "You wish to waltz here?"

Costermongers were pushing handcarts along the muddy thoroughfare. A coach passed by, the roof laden with luggage. Two gentlemen stumbled out of Boodle's Gentlemen's Club, hats askew, and couldn't decide which way to walk home.

"I want to dance with my husband. When I'm with you, no one else exists."

And so that's what they did. They danced the waltz on St James' Street, laughed so hard they mistimed their steps, stopped only to steal a quick kiss. But kissing Benedict always fired lust in her veins, and so they raced home, desperate to find all the possible ways to express their devotion.

CHAPTER SEVENTEEN

Benedict's plan to spend the day in bed lavishing his wife with attention was scuppered by his friends, who descended on Jermyn Street eager to reveal the results of their ongoing investigation.

For the second time in the space of twenty-four hours, Wycliff enjoyed their hospitality while they raced around the bedchamber quickly dressing. Benedict's hair was damp at the nape from their rather energetic lovemaking. Cassandra's lips were swollen from the hours spent locked in a passionate clinch. With their energy spent, they stopped outside the drawing room door to catch their breaths.

"Ah, so no one died this morning," Wycliff said as he rose from the chair flanking the fire while the maid poured tea. "A man might drive himself insane waiting for news that all is well."

Benedict should have called at Bruton Street after the duel, to reassure his friend that Worthen and Tregarth had settled their differences.

"Worthen has a scar on his cheek to match mine, though I doubt the matter is resolved." He waited until Cassandra took a seat on the sofa next to Verity and then squeezed in beside her.

"Worthen stormed from the courtyard and climbed into his carriage without uttering a word. I presume Tregarth joined his friends at The Diamond Club and is probably foxed by now. But forgive me. I should have sent word."

Wycliff settled back into the chair and declined the offer of tea. "No doubt you were both attempting to catch up on missed sleep." Amusement flashed in his dark eyes.

Cassandra tucked a stray lock of hair behind her ear. "Mrs Rampling said you've brought news regarding the investigation." From her hurried tone, she was either desperate to learn the truth or desperate to have this business done with so they might hurry back to the bedchamber.

"We have so much to tell you," Scarlett said from her seat next to her husband. "So much we will be fighting over who should begin."

Benedict dismissed the maid.

Cassandra sat forward. "Do you know who kidnapped me from Lord Craven's ball?"

"Well, no." A look of pity passed over Scarlett's features. "Not precisely." She turned and met Wycliff's gaze. "Explain what happened when you went to visit Lord Craven."

Wycliff straightened. "With Tregarth occupied in fighting a duel, I took it upon myself to visit Craven. The lord was half-cut when I arrived. Bored, he challenged me to a game of hazard which turned into three hours of raucous play. I won. I offered him a means to pay the debt with information. He summoned his household staff and gave me thirty minutes to question them."

Cassandra's eyes widened. "Did you find the maid who went to fetch the smelling salts?"

"She recalls the incident with remarkable clarity," Wycliff continued. "More so because when she returned, your companion had opened the terrace doors, insisting a walk around the grounds was the best course of action. The maid thought it odd because you were dizzy and dragging your feet. But when she suggested finding you a suitable place to rest, the matron helping you snapped at her to leave."

"The matron?" It was Benedict's turn to sit forward and stare with wide eyes. "Lady Murray?" A feeling in his gut told him he was correct in his assumption.

"From the maid's description, I'm certain it was Lady Murray who took care of you in the retiring room."

Cassandra flopped back on the sofa and exhaled a weary sigh. "Then Lady Murray conspired with her son to ensure he had a reason to end our betrothal."

Trent cleared his throat. "Craven's groom remembers a matronly figure assisting a blonde-haired lady into a carriage. Though the matron in question returned to the ballroom."

"My father made a slight detour on his way home." What Wycliff really meant was that his father's journey involved a clandestine meeting. "He saw Lord Murray in the early hours of the morning entering the yard of the Oxford Arms in Warwick Lane. Being preoccupied with his own affair, my father went about his business."

"The Oxford Arms is a coaching inn." A picture of events formed in Benedict's mind. Coaches arrived and departed throughout the night. No one would suspect anything untoward if someone assisted a sleeping woman to a hired room.

Cassandra gestured for Benedict to pass her tea from the trestle table. The teacup rattled on the saucer as she gripped the china. "We discovered that my abductor carried me from Hyde Park Corner down to the Serpentine shortly before dawn," she said, though did not reveal that a vagabond was the source of their information. "The villain must have kept me somewhere during the interim. A coaching inn is an ideal place."

Indeed, it seemed their thoughts were aligned.

Verity turned to face Cassandra. "The evidence suggests that the Murrays snatched you from Lord Craven's ball with the sole purpose of ruining your reputation."

"Then we shall visit the Murrays this afternoon and threaten them until they confess." Benedict's tone was as grave as his intentions. And yet Lord Murray seemed so earnest when he professed his innocence. "What about the woman Purcell bundled into his carriage?"

"Ah, I can help with that," Wycliff said. "Purcell is still a righteous prig, but it seems he may be innocent. Lord Craven informed me that Purcell's mistress arrived at the ball. She drank too much champagne, caused a scene with his wife and so Craven told them to leave. Purcell has been absent from town these last few days as his wife insisted they retire to the country."

Damn. Benedict had wanted an excuse to challenge the pompous lord. He would have loved to wipe the arrogant smirk off Purcell's face.

Cassandra handed her cup and saucer to Benedict, and he placed the china on the table before capturing her hand and stroking her fingers with his thumb.

She squeezed his hand before saying, "Forgive me, but I have a question, Mr Trent."

Trent's gaze dropped to their clasped hands. "Lawrence. Call me Lawrence, or Trent, if you prefer."

Cassandra's countenance brightened. "When the groom told you the matron returned to the ball, did he say if the carriage remained in the mews?"

It was an important question. Lady Murray may have been acting benevolently, providing a safe place for Cassandra to rest while unwell. Someone else might have drugged her drink and waited for an opportune moment to strike.

Trent shook his head and looked thoroughly annoyed with himself. "I assumed the carriage left the mews but did not think to ask for confirmation."

Silence descended, though Benedict could almost hear Trent's mental cursing.

"Murray has an alibi until midnight," Benedict said, "so

someone else must have been inside the carriage with Cassandra."

A sudden knock on the door brought Slocombe. The butler advised Benedict that Miss Atwood had come to call. The news brought a smile to Cassandra's downturned lips, and so he invited the lady to join them for tea. With luck, she might have remembered something important about that fateful night.

Dressed in a black pelisse, and an equally dull bonnet that covered most of her vibrant red hair, the lady bid them good morning. Slocombe drew a chair from the far side of the room and placed it next to the sofa.

"Thank you." Miss Atwood dropped into the seat with a relieved sigh, as if she had raced a mile and needed a moment to fill her lungs. Her nose and cheeks were flushed, drawing attention to the sprinkling of freckles.

"Forgive me, Miss Atwood," Wycliff said, inclining his head respectfully, "are we to offer our condolences?"

The lady frowned. She glanced down at her morbid attire and laughed. "Oh, you speak of my mourning clothes. No, no one has died, Mr Wycliff. This is my disguise."

The comment roused excitement amongst the ladies, and they all shuffled to the edge of their seats.

"A disguise?" Scarlett said, intrigue flashing in her eyes. "May I ask why you feel the need to conceal your identity?"

Miss Atwood shrugged. "It's not a secret. The more people who know, the more likely I am to discover the necessary information." She leaned forward, and everyone in the room followed suit. "I have been stalking Mr Daventry this morning and wished to blend in with the crowd."

Wycliff arched a cautionary brow. "Lucius Daventry?"

"Indeed." Miss Atwood beamed. "Don't tell me. He is reputed to be a devious devil, and I should have a care before I go poking my nose into his affairs."

"Exactly so," Wycliff replied, though he seemed rather amused.

Scarlett gave a knowing grin. "There is only one reason why a lady would stalk a gentleman, Miss Atwood. I kept abreast of my husband's whereabouts for years before I married him."

Miss Atwood snorted. "I am not obsessed with the man if that is your understanding. I simply seek knowledge of the auction he is holding, the auction to dispose of my father's possessions."

Cassandra gave everyone a brief insight into Miss Atwood's problem. "And so, Mr Daventry has refused to grant her a seat at the sale."

"Oh, he's done more than refuse." Miss Atwood's jaw firmed. "He informed me by letter that an auction is no place for a woman. He did not even have the decency to greet me in person. I would call the man a walking monument to misogyny if he hadn't bedded half the ladies in the *ton*."

"Daventry certainly has a love for women," Wycliff countered.

Miss Atwood caught Wycliff's assessing gaze and said, "Yes, and what a shame he finds me disagreeable, else I might have seduced the information from his disreputable lips."

The room fell into a stunned silence.

"Wycliff is right, Miss Atwood," Benedict began. "I speak purely out of concern for your welfare when I say you should approach Daventry with caution."

While the lady might not be considered attractive in the usual sense, there was something fascinating about her character, fascinating enough to be of interest to a gentleman who'd grown bored with insipid beauties. And Daventry might look to seduction as a means to rid himself of a pest.

"You don't know Sybil," Cassandra said with a hint of pride. "Determination is a trait she aspires to."

Miss Atwood nodded in agreement. "Mr Daventry has had me traipsing across town and back again, but I am determined to prove that some women insist on having a voice." She shivered visibly as if an image of Lucius Daventry plagued her mind.

"But that's enough talk of the devilish rogue. And you must forgive me for interrupting your tea."

"We've come together this morning to discuss new information regarding what happened to me at Lord Craven's ball," Cassandra said before relaying their findings. "Despite the mounting evidence, we have no solid proof Lady Murray has behaved deviously."

Miss Atwood pursed her lips. "I see. Then pressing for a confession seems your only course of action."

"I couldn't agree more, Miss Atwood," Trent said.

A sudden frown marred Miss Atwood's brow. "Oh, Lord!" A heavy sigh escaped her. "Perhaps I should have stopped when I saw her this morning, but Mr Daventry had me hopping about from Bloomsbury to Cornhill. She will find herself in a heap of trouble if caught. Lord Murray is likely to run her around in circles."

"Who?" Cassandra asked though the word must have hung on everyone's lips.

"Rosamund." Miss Atwood tutted. "If her aunt discovers she's sneaking about town pestering a peer for a confession, there'll be hell to pay."

Benedict held his breath.

A sense of unease, dread and foreboding descended.

Cassandra gripped his hand. "You saw Rosamund with Lord Murray this morning?" Mistrust dripped from every syllable.

"Yes, about thirty minutes ago." Miss Atwood shook her head again. "I passed by in a hackney as they entered Warwick Lane. It struck me as odd. What need have they to venture to that part of town? But now you've explained the urgency to gain a confession it makes more sense."

It made little sense to Benedict. Judging by the grave look on everyone's faces, it made little sense to them, too.

"I have not seen Rosamund since she ignored me at Lord Tregarth's ball." Pain and confusion coated Cassandra's words now. "Indeed, I cannot think why she would entertain Lord Murray."

"Can you not?" Wycliff spoke with brimming cynicism. "I can think of a reason why a lady might walk towards a coaching inn with a man once betrothed to her friend."

CHAPTER EIGHTEEN

"What if Rosamund blames Lord Murray for what happened to me and means to do him harm?" It sounded an unlikely explanation, but Cassandra was drowning beneath waves of disbelief and had to find something stable to cling on to. "You should have seen her look of mortification when she stumbled upon me in the retiring room."

Their carriage turned into Warwick Lane—a bustling street filled with travellers and tourists and medical men—and came to an abrupt halt outside a butcher's shop with pig carcasses hanging in the window.

Benedict's gaze softened as he considered her from the seat opposite. "Cassandra, while I expect to find Murray and Miss Fox at the coaching inn, the lady hasn't dragged him across town just to reprimand him for ungentlemanly conduct."

The horrible sick feeling churned in her stomach. "Perhaps she believes the lord is guilty and seeks to use gentle persuasion to gain a confession."

"You know better than to fall for such a naive notion. I would wager Murray is the one currently using gentle persuasion." When she slapped her hand to her mouth, Benedict added,

"Forgive me if you find my manner blunt. But I'll not have these people take you for a fool."

"No," she agreed with a sad sigh. "You're right. It's ridiculous to think Rosamund is here to champion my cause." Suspicion reared its ugly head again, forcing her to think the worst. "Do you suppose they have formed an attachment? That they intend to elope, head north of the border?" Why else would they come to a coaching inn?

Benedict crossed the carriage to sit beside her. "Ask yourself why Murray would journey by public coach when he has the benefit of a more luxurious means of transport."

She inhaled a deep breath. The truth would prod and poke her until she straightened and took notice. But how did one summon the worst sort of thoughts about a dear friend?

"Compare Miss Fox's monetary worth to that of Miss Pendleton," he added. "The reason they're here has nothing to do with gaining confessions or proposing marriage. Why do you suppose I asked Wycliff to call on Sir William and bring him to the Oxford Arms?"

When one approached matters from a logical standpoint, as Benedict did, and did not let fragile emotions do the thinking, the reason seemed blatantly obvious.

"Then you suspect Timothy and Rosamund are in love?"

Benedict bent his head and kissed her tenderly on the mouth. "I suspect Miss Fox thinks she's in love. Murray might have other pressing matters on his mind."

She stared into her husband's captivating blue eyes, and the past crept out of its shallow grave to haunt her again. It took immense effort not to tell him she understood what betrayal felt like now. Like the carcasses in the shop window, she was empty inside.

"I trust you're right." She shuffled closer and claimed his mouth in a kiss that banished all maudlin thoughts. "You're my best advisor, my greatest friend. The love of my life."

Benedict seemed surprised by her sudden sentimental

outpouring. He returned her kiss with equal passion. Matters might have progressed further had the carriage not jerked forward on the cobblestones, had they not been out to snare a liar and deceiver.

"I trust no one but you, Benedict."

With gentle strokes, he pushed her hair from her face. "If you want to stop bitterness festering inside, you must trust everyone until they give you a reason to withdraw the privilege. Despite all I have said, we will reserve judgement until faced with the evidence."

She nodded. "Then we shall take our emotions out of the equation and deal with this logically."

"Indeed." He glanced out of the window as the carriage crawled along the lane leading to St Paul's and the College of Physicians. "When we arrive at the inn, I shall visit the office. Honesty is the best policy. I would rather not hammer on every door looking for your fickle friends."

"Agreed."

Neither spoke for a minute, though the din of the street sellers hawking their wares and the cries of frustrated coachmen filled the silence.

Foston steered the carriage along the narrow passageway running west off Warwick Lane. They passed through the red-brick archway into the yard of the Oxford Arms and alighted near the entrance.

"Park here," Benedict advised his coachman. He gestured to the cart and the carriages jostling for a position. "Once the carrier has loaded the cart with packages, you might move closer. Should you see a foppish gentleman attempting to flee, apprehend him."

"Aye, sir."

"And Mr Wycliff should arrive soon. Pay close attention. Watch which room I enter and direct him there."

"Last call for Oxford!" a boy cried, gripping the reins of a team of four as the passengers clambered to take their seats. A door slammed on the second floor of the open gallery, and a fellow appeared, holding his top hat to his head as he raced down the open staircase.

"It's been over an hour since Sybil saw Rosamund heading this way." Cassandra gripped Benedict's arm as they navigated the crowds, dodged the mounds of manure the poor boys struggled to sweep amid the hordes of people. "Even if they came here, they might have left long before now."

Benedict cast her a sidelong glance before steering her around a stable hand taking receipt of a hired horse. "Murray was seen entering the inn on the night you were abducted. He's clearly familiar with the place. There's every reason to suspect Rosamund played a part in your ruination, too."

Nausea plagued her again. She breathed deeply to bolster her courage, inhaled the rank smell of manure and a host of other vile odours which acted as a potent sal volatile.

"Perhaps they left something incriminating behind," he continued, sounding highly doubtful as he led her towards the office, "and having checked the room are long gone. Or perhaps it's a little more complicated than that." From the tone of his voice, he believed it was the latter.

"Sir William will be enraged if we drag him here on a false errand."

Benedict gave a mocking snort. "Sir William will be respectful and polite unless he wishes others to learn of his predilection for tight spaces."

Cassandra shook the image from her head and glanced up at the of row of doors behind the wooden balusters. Washing hung from a makeshift line strung from the timber posts of the galleried inn. A few drunken men lingered near the entrance to the stables, eyeing new arrivals as they stepped from a coach. The place was filthy and rowdy and not at all somewhere one would want to conduct a romantic liaison.

They joined the queue at the office hatch, and it took a few minutes for the attendant to beckon them forward.

"If you're wanting passage on the Oxford stage, you'd best be quick." The woman with grey wiry hair and skin as rough as old leather stared at them across the crude counter. "Well? People are waiting."

Benedict was about to speak, but Cassandra touched his arm. Her husband inclined his head and gestured for her to continue.

"I'm afraid we are here on more serious business." Cassandra held out her hand, and Benedict dropped a few coins into her palm. "A gentleman has taken a young lady with a delicate constitution to one of your rooms." One would hardly consider a woman of Rosamund's deceptive nature delicate. "We wish to speak to them privately before her father arrives and raises a hue and cry."

The woman stared at Cassandra's clenched hand. "Save your coins, dearie. Rules are rules. We don't tattle on our guests. Now move along." She looked behind them and called, "Any more for Oxford?"

Cassandra refused to budge. "I implore you to reconsider."

The woman chuckled, revealing her less than perfect teeth. "Oh, do you hear that? The lady implores me to reconsider."

Benedict stiffened. Cassandra could feel the thrum of his barely contained rage. But it was time to fight her own battles. Time to find the backbone needed when dealing with treachery.

Rousing a lifetime of anger and frustration, she slammed the coin on the counter. "Tell me what blasted room they are in else I shall storm upstairs and kick down every door until I find them." Blood boiled in her veins. "Then I shall consult my dear friend in the licensing office and do my utmost to get yours revoked."

The woman's arrogant grin faded.

"Trust me," Cassandra continued. "You will have one hell of a fight on your hands. Indeed, perhaps you would prefer to pay a fine for late mail, as I shall gather a band of rioters to ensure none of your coaches leave on time."

There was something rather empowering about ranting in a

public place. She might have threatened to rouse the devil, too, but the woman behind the counter heaved a sigh of surrender.

Cassandra leaned forward. "I shall start by telling everyone in this yard that you condone the abuse of young women."

The woman threw them a deadly stare. "What does she look like, this young woman?"

Cassandra described the two conspirators she had once thought of as friends. "They arrived here an hour ago," she snapped. "But that is not the first time they have used your establishment to conduct their secret *meetings*."

The gentle touch of Benedict's hand on her back worked to calm her temper. "If you could tell us which room they've occupied," he said, "we shall address the matter with the minimum of fuss and disruption."

The woman shook her head and muttered to herself. She snatched a ledger and ran a grubby finger down the scrawled list on the page. "Second floor, first room to the right of the stairs." With her beady eyes trained on them, she seized the coins and shouted, "Any more for Oxford?"

Benedict guided Cassandra to the stairs, and they mounted the steps with haste. She took a moment to catch her breath while hovering outside the door—the only barrier between her and the ugly truth.

Again, Benedict was about to knock, but she said, "Allow me."

He inclined his head. "Remember, it is better to face facts than live with falsehoods. Together, we will deal with whatever we discover beyond this door."

Feeling an overpowering love for her husband, she clutched his lapels and pressed a kiss to his lips. "When this is over, I shall spend a lifetime showing you how much I love you."

Benedict arched a brow. "Then knock the damn door as I am desperate to feel the depth of your devotion."

She smiled, lifted her chin, knocked the door and in an accent common in the streets of Whitechapel said, "Coach is leavin' for Oxford. Best hurry. They're waitin' for yer to take yer place."

Silence ensued.

She knocked louder. "Driver said he'll come up 'ere and drag yer out if yer make him late."

A bang on the boards beyond told them the room was occupied.

"You've got the wrong room. Check your damn records."

Benedict met Cassandra's gaze. "Without a doubt that's Murray." His mouth thinned into a savage line.

"Indeed." Anger infused her tone when she hammered again and said, "The next one's not for three days. Brutus ain't the sort who likes to be kept waitin'." She thumped the door twice.

Benedict pressed his ear to the door. "I can hear movement and a lot of cursing. Stand aside as we might need to barge our way in."

Cassandra shuffled right. Benedict squared his shoulders and waited for Lord Murray to open the door.

The pad of footsteps preceded the rattle of the doorknob. In a fit of temper, Murray yanked open the door. Shock rendered him mute. His jaw sagged, and he staggered back.

Benedict barged into the room. Cassandra quickly followed and slammed the door shut. The feminine cry drew her gaze to the bed, to Rosamund who clutched the faded coverlet to her naked breasts and stared at them with incredulous eyes.

"Rosamund. How lovely to see you." This time Cassandra had no intention of drawing her friend into an embrace.

"C-Cassandra." Rosamund shuffled in the bed. "I—I can explain."

Lord Murray—dressed in nothing but a loose linen shirt and breeches—finally found his voice and said, "What the devil" before Benedict punched the lord so hard in the face he dropped to the floor like a lead weight.

Satisfaction thrummed in Cassandra's veins. "Your knuckles! You need to let them heal."

Benedict flexed his fingers and winced. "Remind me to visit Jackson's Salon and practise my left hook." He looked at Lord Murray writhing on the floor, clutching his nose. "Stay down else I shall hit you again."

Cassandra turned her attention to the minx in the bed. "Well? Let me hear your explanation, Rosamund. Tell me how long you have been the bed partner of the man I was supposed to marry. And don't lie to me. Not now."

Rosamund whimpered.

"Don't say anything," Lord Murray interjected before Benedict kicked him in the knee and roused a howl.

Cassandra arched a brow. "I'm waiting."

"Three months," her disloyal friend mumbled into the shabby coverlet.

"Three months!"

Betrayal dug the pointed tip of its blade into Cassandra's heart. She had confided in Rosamund, spoken about the lord's reluctance to set a wedding date. Rosamund had smiled and offered words of comfort and reassurance. Had given her every reason to believe she cared.

"Is that why you suggested I might be better suited to someone other than Timothy?" She turned her attention to the deceitful lord sprawled on the dusty boards. "And you professed to love me. You pretended to be above those obsessed with the sins of the flesh. Why agree to marry me if you were in love with someone else?"

"Surely you know the answer," Rosamund said feebly, speaking on the lord's behalf as if they were already a married couple. "You agreed to marry Timothy despite the fact you were in love with Mr Cavanagh."

Cassandra's temper eased upon hearing the truth. "Because my father gave me no option, and because I thought I had lost the love of my life."

"We wanted to tell you," Rosamund said, sniffing back tears, "but we didn't want to hurt you. So many times, I have wanted to confess. Love makes people do reckless things."

"Love?" Benedict gave a mocking snort. "Murray suggested Cassandra might become his mistress now she's married. Does that sound like love to you?"

Rosamund's eyes grew wide. "You must have misunderstood." She shook her head. "We're in love and will marry as soon as Timothy persuades his mother to agree."

The oaf on the floor remained silent.

"Lady Murray will never agree. Murray knows that." Benedict grabbed the poor excuse of a man by the scruff of his shirt and hauled him to his feet. "Tell her about your ridiculous spending habit. Tell her that your mother wishes you to marry Miss Pendleton. That money will be your only motivation when you marry. Tell her you had a hand in my wife's ruination so you could marry a lady whose father is generous with his purse."

"How many more times do you want me to tell you?" Lord Murray protested. "I had nothing to do with what happened to Cassandra."

Rosamund gripped the coverlet and straightened. "Does Mr Cavanagh speak the truth? Does your mother want you to marry Miss Pendleton?"

"Well, yes, she suggested Miss Pendleton might be a good match," Lord Murray said with some exasperation. "But I intend to persuade her otherwise."

The man was lying through his teeth.

"If you had nothing to do with my abduction, what were you doing here at the Oxford Arms on the night in question?" Someone had watched over her before depositing her in Hyde Park. "Whoever kidnapped me held me captive for hours before executing their plan. We have witnesses claiming your mother bundled me into a carriage." Anger surfaced again at the thought of her mistreatment. "You drugged my lemonade. You stayed at the ball so you would have an alibi."

"That's ridiculous, all conjecture."

"The Marquis of Blackbeck saw you enter this establishment in the early hours," Benedict snapped, "and will claim so publicly." With a claw-like grip, he grabbed Lord Murray by the throat. "I'll have your confession if it's the last thing I do."

The lord croaked as his face turned beetroot red.

"Wait!" Rosamund cried. "Timothy met me here that night. I managed to escape my father's house and hired a hackney. So you see, he had nothing to do with the kidnapping."

Despite Rosamund's plea, Benedict refused to release the lord. "Then you acted as his accomplice. You both kept Cassandra here and waited for dawn to approach. Lady Murray played her part because she thought her son wanted an excuse to marry Miss Pendleton and knew nothing of his affair with you. You helped him ruin the lady you called your friend."

Murray punched Benedict's arm as he gasped for air.

"No! Let him go!" Rosamund came up on her knees while clutching the coverlet. She focused her frantic gaze on Cassandra. "I tried to help you. I did the only thing I could when I learned of their wicked plot."

The world stopped.

Cassandra's heart missed multiple beats.

Every bone in her body stiffened as Rosamund's words took shape in her mind. More lies. More treachery. More deceit.

Benedict released the hypocritical lord, and Murray collapsed to his knees and heaved. "You had better tell us everything you know else you will rue the day you ever met me."

Tears sprang in Rosamund's eyes. Guilt marred her pretty features. "Timothy spoke the truth when he said he knew nothing of what happened." She dashed the water from her eyes. "On the night of Lord Craven's ball, after you'd gone to rest in the retiring room, I took the opportunity to meet Timothy in the library."

"You mean you used my illness to your advantage."

"We stole every available moment to spend time together."

Blessed saints!

How had she ever believed this woman was her friend?

How had she been so blind?

"I thought Rosamund said the music room," the lord informed them as he found the strength to clamber to his feet. "I waited there for thirty minutes."

"So, you were waiting in the library for Murray to show," Benedict prompted in a tone that would make most men fear for their lives.

Rosamund hung her head. "I always hide behind the curtain while waiting, in case my aunt should come looking. When the door opened and closed, I peered through the gap to check it was Timothy, but it was Lady Murray who entered."

"My mother!" The lord's confused tone suggested he was oblivious to the matron's involvement.

"Lady Murray started pacing the floor, wringing her hands and muttering to herself. She hurried to the decanters, poured something potent into a glass and swallowed it quickly." Rosamund paled. "Someone else slipped into the room. Someone Lady Murray had agreed to meet."

"Who?" Cassandra held her breath.

"Your father."

"Lord Worthen?" Benedict clearly needed clarification.

"Yes."

"What the devil?" Lord Murray seemed as interested as they were upon hearing this sudden revelation. "What was the purpose of their meeting?"

Tears trickled down Rosamund's cheeks. "It seems they were tired of waiting for you to set a wedding date. They both wanted you to marry and so had set a plan in motion that would see you forced to wed."

Confusion clouded Cassandra's mind.

Was there no one she could trust?

"Lady Murray added a tincture to your drink. She managed to get you into a hired carriage where her lady's maid was waiting to escort you to a meeting point near Green Park." A convenient location as it was a stone's throw from Hyde Park. "The earl confirmed that he would meet the carriage after leaving the ball and continue with his part of the plan."

The truth proved excruciating. Proved too much to bear.

Clutching her chest in a bid to stop the savage stabbing in her heart, Cassandra crumpled to the floor. A wracking sob took command of her body, and she cried so hard she struggled to catch her breath. A title did not give someone the right to play God with people's lives. A parent should be loving and supportive, not spiteful and vindictive.

Benedict crouched beside her and wrapped his arm around her shoulders. "It is better to release your pain. No one will ever hurt you like this again. I give you my word."

"Did you not think to inform someone of the plot?" Lord Murray asked as if he were fighting their corner, too. "Good God, Rosamund, we could have prevented this whole fiasco. No doubt my mother was coerced into behaving so abominably."

"I'm sorry," Rosamund cried. "But don't you see, it gave us all an opportunity to live as we wanted. Had I not intervened, you would be married to Cassandra, and like me, Mr Cavanagh would be nursing a broken heart."

Cassandra wiped away her tears. She clutched Benedict's arm and came to her feet. "What do you mean you intervened?"

Rosamund gulped, and it took her a moment to gather her wits. "Lady Murray paid a boy to deliver anonymous letters to prominent people. Timothy was to arrive in Hyde Park first. The others were to follow shortly afterwards. Lady Murray was to encourage Timothy to go to the park at the appointed time."

"But I didn't receive a letter," the lord replied.

"No, because you were here with me. When they left the library, I used Lord Craven's desk and wrote a letter to Mr Cavanagh." Rosamund turned her attention to Cassandra. "You pointed out his house once if you remember, and so I had a boy deliver my letter to Mr Cavanagh and made sure Timothy wasn't at home to receive his."

"I was three parts foxed and didn't leave the inn until nine the next morning," Lord Murray said, and then recognition dawned. "My mother was pacing the floor, frantic when I eventually arrived home."

A tense silence descended.

With her mind chaotic, Cassandra didn't know how to feel, how to react. Regardless of her friendly protestations, Rosamund's motive stemmed from selfish desires. Lord Murray was a decadent pleasure-seeker. In playing a devious game, he had been manipulated, too. The couple deserved each other, deserved to live a life filled with doubt and mistrust.

"Don't expect my gratitude, Rosamund. You made so many assumptions, took so many chances with my life. What if Benedict hadn't married me? What if I'd been forced to marry a man old enough to be my grandfather?"

Before Rosamund could reply, a knock on the door stole their attention. The series of raps reminded Cassandra of the complicated code used to gain access to Mrs Crandall's abode, and most certainly signalled Damian Wycliff's arrival.

Benedict took hold of her hand and whispered, "You've had enough upset for one day. I'm taking you home." He cast his stone-like gaze on Lord Murray and Rosamund. "Well, when in Rome, do as the Romans do. You're not the only ones who like to manipulate situations to their advantage."

Benedict opened the door and bid Mr Wycliff and Sir William entry.

"So, it's as we expected." Mr Wycliff's smirk stretched from ear to ear as Sir William tore into the room as if the devil were at his heels.

"I'll explain later," Benedict said amid the cries and sudden shouting, "but for now I'm taking Cassandra home."

Mr Wycliff inclined his head. "I shall call on you in Jermyn Street and inform you of what occurs here."

The fracas spilling out of the room drew the gazes of everyone in the courtyard. No one gave Cassandra and Benedict a second glance as they strolled through the stunned crowd back to their carriage. All eyes were upon the lord being dragged onto the gallery, wearing nothing but his shirt and breeches.

Neither of them spoke as they settled into the carriage seat. Cassandra rested her head on Benedict's shoulder, sleep and the need to make love to her husband being the overriding thoughts. Indeed, they would tackle the matter of her father and Lady Murray in due course.

And then there would be hell to pay.

CHAPTER NINETEEN

Tregarth owned many warehouses surrounding the London Docks in Wapping. New storage facilities built to house luxury commodities such as silk and spices. Modern buildings. Elegant buildings. But one did not indulge cruel people, and so the setting for a night of mischief and mayhem was a small warehouse beyond the murky street of Lower Shadwell. A place frequented by thieves and drunken sailors, men comfortable with criminal activity.

"Is it possible to feel terrified and excited at the same time?" Cassandra sat on a wooden crate while Benedict lit the oil lamps hanging from metal chains flung over the rafters.

"You've spent a lifetime playing the obedient daughter. Now it's time to make your own rules, follow your own destiny."

Her smile warmed his heart. "People reap what they sow. I only hope my abductors feel the same sense of desperate despair as I did when I woke in the park wearing nothing but a filthy chemise."

Benedict scanned the damp brick building, wondering what Lady Murray and the Earl of Worthen would make of their prison when they arrived. The air was pungent with the smell of tobacco and the potent fumes from rum. The scurrying of rats searching for food had Cassandra continually looking over her shoulder.

There were no windows.

No doors, bar one.

No means of escape.

"I have lost count of how many times I have asked," she said, drawing the thick cloak across her chest, "but have we much longer to wait?"

Benedict pulled his watch from his pocket and inspected the face beneath the light of the lamp. "It's ten o'clock. The first of our prisoners should be here soon."

Tregarth, Wycliff and Trent were tasked with stealing the earl from his home and bringing him to the dingy warehouse. The Marquis of Blackbeck, Scarlett and Verity had the pleasure of escorting Lady Murray to the place of inquisition.

Cassandra stood and brushed dust off her cloak. "My pulse is racing so fast it's drumming in my ears."

He closed the gap between them and drew her into an embrace. "If there was justice in the world, we would strip both conspirators of their good names and leave them to rot in a squalid gaol." But the law protected manipulative men like Worthen. It protected cunning ladies who sought to control people's lives, too.

Cassandra came up on her toes and kissed him tenderly on the lips. "Banishing them from London is the best we can hope for."

"Trust me. They will never harm you again."

"I owe Sybil a great deal. Had she not mentioned seeing Rosamund in Warwick Lane, we would have been forever chasing our tails."

He caressed her cheek and gave a knowing smirk. "I will speak to Daventry on her behalf, though I pray you will caution Miss Atwood in the folly of pursuing a man with such a notorious reputation."

A light laugh breezed from her lips. "Sybil has a will of her own. Woe betide anyone who tries to tell her what to do."

"She's a good friend." Upon learning of Miss Fox's duplicity, Miss Atwood had been eager to reassure Cassandra that she knew nothing of their friend's affair with Murray. "And we will assist her in any way we can."

The sound of footsteps outside drew their attention to the door. The series of knocks that played like a melody confirmed Wycliff's arrival.

Benedict rushed forward, slid the bolts and opened the door. Gripping an arm each, Wycliff and Trent dragged the Earl of Worthen into the old building. Tregarth followed, wielding a stick sword, the tip of which he took pleasure prodding in Worthen's back.

Cassandra's face turned ashen. It was one thing to imagine exacting revenge, another to see it played out before one's eyes.

"Get your bloody hands off me!" Worthen struggled to free himself, but no man was as strong as Trent. "I swear, heads will roll for this." Through red, puffy eyes, he glared at Benedict. "Don't think your father will save you this time."

Cassandra rushed forward. "Silence! I've heard enough of your nonsense to last a lifetime. The only person who needs saving is you."

Worthen blinked in shock at his daughter's sudden outburst. "Look what he's done to you. Did I not tell you, heathens corrupt the soul? You should have married Murray."

"Lord Murray is bedding Miss Fox." Cassandra braced her hands on her hips. "For three months they have been sneaking about behind my back. Is that the sort of man you want for my husband?"

Worthen scoffed. "Every man partakes in the odd dalliance."

"Not every man," Benedict countered. He dragged a crude chair and placed it in the middle of the room. "Now sit down, before I knock you down."

Trent and Wycliff pushed the lord into the chair. Tregarth

played prison guard and kept the tip of his sword pointed at the earl's non-existent heart.

"Well?" Worthen barked at Tregarth. "I should have known you'd go back on your word." The lord was so misguided, was such a damn hypocrite, it was laughable. "We fought a duel over the attack on your son. Why the devil have you brought me here?"

"You can stop pretending." Benedict came to stand in front of Worthen and folded his arms across his chest. "You expect us to believe you have not spoken to your good friend Lady Murray?"

Eight hours had passed since Benedict had brought Cassandra home from their enlightening trip to the Oxford Arms. Sir William would have called on Lady Murray as a matter of urgency. Therefore, she must know what had transpired.

"Good friend? The woman is a backstabbing termagant. A demon in pearls. A conniving devil."

"A conniving devil?" Cassandra came to stand before the earl, too. "Is that not the reason you conspired with her to bring about my ruination? Perhaps you were unaware that Miss Fox was hiding behind the curtain in Lord Craven's library when the two of you discussed your despicable plan."

Worthen gulped a breath as the words penetrated, as it suddenly dawned on him why he'd been abducted from his home and brought to a decrepit warehouse.

A tense silence ensued.

Tregarth drew the tip of the blade up to Worthen's throat. "Well? We're waiting to hear your explanation, George."

Another series of knocks on the door signalled the arrival of the other devious player in this game. Trent assisted Verity and Scarlett in hauling the disgruntled matron into the ramshackle building. The Marquis of Blackbeck followed behind. The arrogant smirk on his face suggested he was enjoying the night's proceedings.

Dressed immaculately in black, the marquis waited as Scarlett forced the matron into the chair next to Lord Worthen and then said, "When I perused my diary this week, I do not recall seeing abduction on the list of appointments."

Wycliff glanced at his father. "Don't pretend you're not excited at the prospect of watching events unfold."

"Yes, almost as excited as poor Lady Murray when her butler informed her a marquis had come to call."

"This is an outrage!" Lady Murray's cheeks flamed red. "I demand you return me to Mortimer Street at once." Her irate gaze scanned her abductors. "Do you know who I am?"

Blackbeck stepped forward. His amused grin faded. "You most certainly know who I am, madam, and you do not want to feel the full force of my wrath."

The matron turned her anger on Lord Worthen. "What the devil have you told them? Doubtless it's all lies. More fictitious drivel."

"You're the bare-faced liar," Worthen countered. "There is little point playing innocent now. I should have known you had hidden motives when you devised the blasted plan."

"Me?" The matron clutched her chest, affronted. "Me! You're the heartless fool who uses his own daughter to further his ends."

"I guarantee, people would have paid a fortune to watch this show," Blackbeck interjected. "It reminds me of an opera I once saw in—"

"This is a serious matter," Wycliff snapped. "If you wish to play your part, you will watch the performance quietly from the stalls."

Blackbeck inclined his head in acquiescence. "Then I shall brace myself for the finale."

Benedict cleared his throat and regaled the tale told to them by Rosamund Fox. He then informed Lady Murray that a witness had placed her in the retiring room with Cassandra. That a witness saw her bundle Cassandra into a carriage in the mews.

"Without doubt, you are both to blame." Cassandra's cold tone conveyed her feelings for the perpetrators of the crime. "And yet when one examines the facts, there are discrepancies in the tale."

Benedict frowned, curious as to his wife's train of thought.

"Father," she began, the word full of contempt. "I am in no doubt you caused me untold anguish, that you planned to force Timothy to marry me quickly. Then you would champion his ambitions in government and use him for your own devious ends."

A tense silence hung in the air while everyone waited for Cassandra to continue. Indeed, the earl did not deny the accusation.

"But you, Lady Murray, your actions are at odds with what I know of your character."

The matron shook her head. "I haven't the first clue what you mean."

"Let us suppose you wanted Timothy to marry quickly in the hope of controlling his outrageous spending. Let us all agree that you are guilty of orchestrating my ruination. All for your beloved son's benefit I might add."

"Is it wrong to want the best for one's offspring?"

"Not at all, which is why I cannot believe you would arrange for influential men like Lord Purcell to arrive at the Serpentine to witness your son's disgrace. You want him to be a man of power and position and yet being caught supposedly compromising me would harm his reputation amongst his peers."

Benedict absorbed the information and had to agree with Cassandra's assessment.

"Peasants frolic in the park," Blackbeck muttered from his position at the back. "When a gentleman of refinement seduces a woman, he does so with a little more finesse."

"Precisely," Cassandra said, keeping her gaze trained on Lady Murray. "And so you had my father assist in your plan knowing you had no intention of giving your son the letter, knowing those gentlemen would find me alone in the park and then your son would have good cause to end our betrothal."

Worthen's face twisted in fury. "You … you evil witch!" The blade at his throat prevented him from jumping to his feet.

Lady Murray smirked. "You must admit, I had you fooled right to the very end."

"Except that you knew nothing of your son's affair with Miss Fox," Cassandra added. No one had suspected that. "Rosamund had her own reasons for intervening. She sent the letter to Benedict knowing he would arrive in your son's place."

Benedict scoffed. "And now Murray will have no option but to marry Miss Fox, a woman lacking the funds necessary to ease the burden of his excessive spending."

A chuckle escaped the matron's lips. "You think my need to sever ties with the earl stemmed from worries about money? Piffle! I conspired to keep my son from being used to further Lord Worthen's ends."

And there it was.

The bare truth of the matter.

As cold and as stark as the bitter night air.

"Judas!" Worthen unleashed a torrent of abuse from his chair. "You'll pay dearly for this, you old trot. I shall spend the rest of my life finding ways to punish your pathetic son."

While everyone watched the hullabaloo, Cassandra breathed a sigh and stepped back. Benedict caught her in his arms as her shoulders sagged and knees buckled.

"Make no mistake, my love," he whispered, pressing a kiss to her temple, "we are the victors in this game. Their meddling brought us together. For that, I shall always be grateful."

She looked up and gently cupped his bruised cheek. "I love you. There is no man in this world as honourable as you."

Despite a room full of witnesses, Benedict would have kissed her, had Lady Murray not jumped to her feet and cried, "Enough of this nonsense! I'll not sit here and be insulted by this whore's bully. I insist you take me home at once."

Cassandra smiled as her hand slipped from Benedict's cheek and came to rest on his chest. "Would you like to deliver the bad news, or shall I?"

"While I would like nothing more than to knock the arrogant smirks off both their faces, I think you should show them that you're not a woman who takes treachery lightly."

Mischief danced in her eyes. She squared her shoulders and swung around to face Lady Murray. "I hate to be the one to tell you this, but Mortimer Street won't be your home for much longer."

A storm of protest commanded the matron's countenance. "Step out of my way else I shall—"

"Shall do what?" Cassandra countered. "Send for a constable and have Lord Blackbeck and Lord Tregarth inform the authorities that you drugged and kidnapped the daughter of an earl? I think not."

The matron's frantic gaze darted about the room. "I shall make a counterclaim, accuse them of kidnapping me from my home."

"Do not dare threaten me, madam." From a dim corner of the room, Blackbeck gave a low growl. "While I've found watching the performance somewhat entertaining, tell me this is my cue to take centre stage."

Cassandra motioned for the lord to step forward. He did so with the grace and sophistication of a man confident in his ability to breeze through a room and create utter devastation.

"It seems your son may have earned a coveted position in government after all." The marquis straightened his cuffs and grinned, though his dark eyes made him look positively wicked. "Lord Liverpool is a personal friend and is seeking a spokesman to assist in foreign affairs. Indeed, we need a representative in Greece to show our support for their war of independence against the Ottoman Empire."

"Greece?" The matron blanched.

"There's no need to thank me. Indeed, I met with your son a

few hours ago at Sir William's house, and he accepted the position with good grace." What he meant was Murray daren't refuse. "Miss Fox will accompany him, of course. Indeed, I hear they have plans to marry posthaste."

"Greece!" Lady Murray repeated.

"The climate is hotter than you're used to, but I am sure you will adjust."

"Me?" An incredulous grin spread from ear to ear. "Why would I want to travel to Greece?"

Through ruthless eyes, Blackbeck stared down his nose, and one imagined hearing an earthly rumble as the ground shook beneath one's feet. "Whether you want to accompany your son to Greece or not, madam, you will sail at the end of the week. Travel arrangements have been made. Your maid is packing as we speak. Unless you would like Lord Liverpool to inform the king of your treachery."

Looking dazed and bewildered and utterly defeated, the matron flopped down into the seat.

Worthen snorted. "And what devious plan do you have for me?" The earl sounded confident he had the wherewithal to tackle whatever was thrown his way.

"You will retire to your estate in Yorkshire," Cassandra said, "where I hope your life will be as bleak as the wind, as desolate as the moorland. You will remain there indefinitely, and never set foot in London again."

"That's preposterous." Worthen glared at her as if she were muck on his boot. "Is that how you treat the man who raised you?"

It took every effort for Benedict to keep his fists at his sides.

"You gave up the right to be my father the day you conspired to have me kidnapped and left me half-naked in Hyde Park." Her voice broke on a sob. "I shall never forgive you for that."

"What? And so you will have Blackbeck threaten me, too?"

"No," Benedict growled through gritted teeth. "I will give you an ultimatum." He ignored the contempt swimming in the earl's eyes. "You see, I have proof you committed fraud. I have copies of certain documents relating to a matter you'd rather I not mention in front of witnesses." He referred to copies of the clerk's letters he had traded with Mrs Crandall in exchange for information relating to Lady Murray's and Miss Fox's devilish deeds. "I have a copy of the letter sent from your man of business issuing instructions. I have a statement from a certain person's sister explaining how you threatened to evict her from her home."

Worthen's cheeks ballooned. "Slanderous drivel. The lot of it!"

Benedict reached into his coat pocket and withdrew a letter given to him by Mrs Crandall. He peeled back the folds and held it up to the earl. "The name of your victim is written plainly." The clerk's name appeared at the top of the missive. "He acted under duress, after being forced to do your bidding. What I have in my possession is substantial proof of your duplicity."

Worthen took one look at the letter, and his ruddy cheeks turned ashen.

"Do anything to hurt Cassandra again," Benedict continued, "and I shall see that Blackbeck delivers the letters to Lord Liverpool." The need to erase every unspoken threat from his memory, every moment where he'd lacked the strength of his conviction, forced him to say, "Out of love, my father prevented me from issuing a formal challenge. Because he knows I wouldn't hesitate to put a lead ball between your brows. Be warned. Continue to cause problems, and I shall do everything in my power to be rid of you for good."

Tregarth prodded Worthen with the tip of his sword. "You have until dawn to leave town. I shall park my carriage in Cavendish Square and escort you to the Great North Road myself."

Knowing his back was pressed to the wall, Worthen took his frustration out on Lady Murray. "By God, this is all your fault.

Don't think you can hide from me in Greece. There's not a place in this world you can go where I won't find you."

While the two heartless fiends continued to quarrel, Cassandra turned to Benedict. "Come. We have wasted enough time on those who are undeserving of our attention. Let's go home. Your father and the marquis will deal with them now."

Tregarth lowered his sword. "I suggest we all return to Jermyn Street and drain Benedict's decanters. I have a few hours before I need to play watchman at Worthen's door."

When at home, excessive drinking was not Benedict's activity of choice. The need to make love to his wife burned hot in his veins. But after the distress of the last few days, being amongst good friends helped to nourish the spirit. Besides, he would have his wife to himself on the carriage ride home.

He turned to face the woman he had loved for as long as he could remember. "If you're tired and would prefer—"

"No, it will be good to spend time with those who have helped champion our cause."

With them all in agreement, Blackbeck escorted Scarlett and Verity from the damp warehouse. Trent set about blowing out the lamps before accompanying Wycliff and Tregarth to the door.

The two devils sitting on the chairs rose nervously to their feet.

"I hope never to lay eyes on the two of you again," Benedict said, draping his arm around Cassandra's shoulder as they made to leave, too.

"Wh-what about us?" Lady Murray protested. "How are we to get home?"

Benedict glanced behind and grinned. "You like concocting plans, like conspiring in dark places. I'm sure you will think of something."

CHAPTER TWENTY

Cassandra rubbed the jasmine-scented bar soap along the length of her arm as she lounged in the bathtub in front of the fire. Ten times she had repeated the action hoping to attract Benedict's attention as he sat propped against a mound of pillows in bed.

"Anything of interest in the broadsheets?" Her desire to have her husband join her in the tub was surely evident in her tone. The water was almost cold. Her fingers and toes were wrinkled. Perhaps it was time to be less subtle.

Benedict scanned the page while snatching a piece of toast from the silver tray on the bed. "Not unless you wish to purchase an Arabian stallion or attend a floral display hosted by the Botanical Society. Nothing to match the excitement we've experienced."

"Do you speak of our chase about town to catch villains or of our rampant sessions in bed?"

"Both." He took a bite of toast and continued to stare at the page. "It's been one hell of a week."

One hell of a week, indeed!

With all the lies and deceit behind them, they could focus on what mattered most. Love, and building a happy future together. Her father was hundreds of miles away in Yorkshire. The marquis had secured a special licence for Lord Murray to marry quickly, and so Rosamund, Timothy and Lady Murray were in Portsmouth awaiting passage to Greece.

"I'm meeting Scarlett and Verity at noon." That would leave just enough time for a little morning play before she had to dress and make her way to Oxford Street. "Sybil might join us if she's not darting about town stalking Mr Daventry."

"Oh, on the subject of Daventry," he said, daring to glance up from the broadsheet. "I saw him briefly last night when visiting Mrs Crandall."

"You did? Why didn't you mention it before?"

He had gone to Theobolds Road with Mr Wycliff and Mr Trent as part of the agreement made when Mrs Crandall gave them the clerk's letters. The madam wished to know what had occurred in the damp warehouse. A secret in exchange for a secret.

"Daventry was entering the premises as we were leaving. We exchanged no more than a few sentences." A sinful grin formed on his lips. "As for not mentioning it before, you were in a rather amorous mood when I returned home if you recall."

She seemed to be in an amorous mood most of the time.

But when one had suffered heartbreak, when one thought their love was lost to them, they grasped every chance of happiness.

"Did you ask about the auction?" Now she had his attention, she raised her leg and took extra care washing her limbs.

Benedict watched her attend to her ablutions for a few seconds before saying, "I mentioned you were friends with Miss Atwood and that the lady had heard he was selling her father's curiosities."

"Excellent. What did he say?"

"Are you sure you want to know?" He folded the newspaper and placed it on the bed.

"Of course I want to know." Although talk of her friend's frustrations was beginning to dampen her ardour. "Sybil is desperate to regain possession of her father's belongings."

"As one would expect from a notorious rake, he said something highly inappropriate."

"Inappropriate?" She waited and when he neglected to divulge the details, said, "Something about Sybil?"

Benedict nodded. "You really want to know?"

"Yes."

Her husband grinned. "He said if she were anyone else, he would have had her impressive breasts in his hands long before now. He even made a gesture to support his claim. He said if you wish for her to remain intact, you should do everything possible to discourage her in her present course."

Good Lord!

Perhaps Sybil needed a chaperone on her outings about town. "If she were anyone else?" Cassandra repeated Mr Daventry's comment aloud. "What did he mean?"

Benedict shrugged, drawing her gaze to his bare chest. "I suspect he dislikes ladies with red hair."

"The man is a self-proclaimed scoundrel. Is one lady not the same as another when frolicking in the dark?"

"Be thankful Sybil isn't his type, else she might lose something more important than her father's possessions."

"Nothing is more important to her than the return of Atticus Atwood's journals and scientific equipment." That's what proved worrying. Sybil laughed in the face of danger, and with no family to offer protection, she was like a sitting duck to men with immoral intentions.

Lost in thought regarding Sybil's troubling situation, Cassandra absently soaped her arms again.

"Why don't you just ask me?" Benedict's biceps bulged as he lounged back against the pillows and folded his arms behind his head. "You know you want to."

"Ask you what? Are you speaking of Sybil and Mr Daventry?"

"No." Mischief danced in his eyes. "Why don't you ask me to squeeze into the bathtub so you may ride me in the wild way you love?"

Heat rose to her cheeks. She had spent half an hour trying to tempt a reaction only for him to come straight to the point. There was no use denying what she blatantly wanted. "Ladies are more discreet than gentlemen when it comes to seduction."

He laughed. "Caressing your body in the tub is hardly considered discreet."

"Washing and caressing are two entirely different things."

"Indeed, you've washed your body once and teased me a handful of times." Naked, he climbed out of bed and padded across the room. "Have you thought that I might like to hear you speak salaciously? That I might find it highly arousing to have my wife tell me she wants me to fill her full?"

She arched a coy brow while deliberately soaping her breasts. "You would rather that than me tell you I love you?"

"You're the love of my life. Every second of the day, I have to pinch myself to make sure I'm not dreaming. Making love is a natural way of letting me know that you need me, desire me, love me. You should never be afraid to ask."

She drank in the sight of his glorious body. "I need you, desire you and love you. I never want to be without you. I love you so much I could burst. But some things are easier to say than others."

"We've spent five years not saying what we mean. Don't be shy. Not with me." He moistened his lips and took himself in hand. "Now, what did you want to say?"

Love and lust burned in her veins. She swallowed deeply. "Join with me."

"I need a little more than that."

"Let me straddle you in the tub and take you into my body."

"A little more."

She moistened her lips. “I don’t think I can last another second without the feel of you thrusting inside me.”

“You see.” He palmed his growing erection and smiled. “Majestic things grow from small beginnings. You taught me that.”

THANK YOU!

Thank you for reading ***When Scandal Came to Town***

Does Sybil Atwood discover the location of Mr Daventry's secret auction?

And what is the devilish gentleman hiding?

Find out in ***The Mystery of Mr Daventry***
Scandalous Sons - Book 4

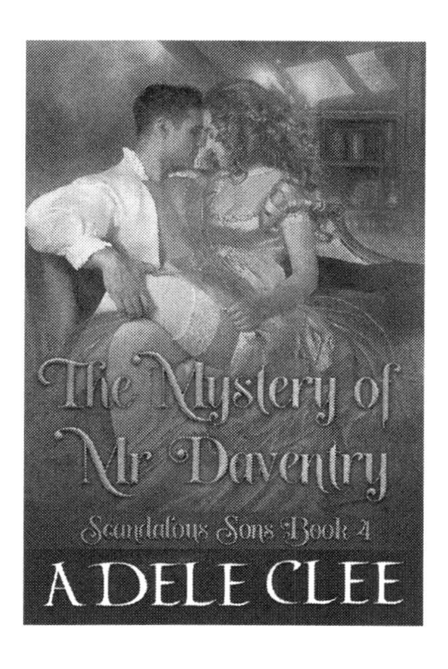

Books by Adele Clee

To Save a Sinner

A Curse of the Heart

What Every Lord Wants

The Secret To Your Surrender

A Simple Case of Seduction

Anything for Love Series

What You Desire

What You Propose

What You Deserve

What You Promised

Lost Ladies of London

The Mysterious Miss Flint

The Deceptive Lady Darby

The Scandalous Lady Sandford

The Daring Miss Darcy

Avenging Lords

At Last the Rogue Returns

A Wicked Wager

Valentine's Vow

A Gentleman's Curse

Scandalous Sons

And the Widow Wore Scarlet

The Mark of a Rogue

When Scandal Came to Town

The Mystery of Mr Daventry

Printed in Great Britain
by Amazon

38306916R00130

Can a past betrayal ever be forgiven?

A shocking surprise awaits him at the Serpentine

When Benedict Cavanagh, the illegitimate son of the Earl Tregarth, discovers the lady he was once destined to marry ly half-naked and ruined in Hyde Park at dawn, his conscie demands he does something to save her. He might have spiri her home before the first riders took to the Row, but the vill behind the staged ruination had other evil plans.

A lady used as a pawn in a wicked game.

The last thing Cassandra Mills deserved was Benedict Cavanag kindness and compassion. Five years had passed since professed her love and promised to marry him. Five years passed since she buckled beneath the weight of responsibility a rejected the handsome rogue. But when she finds herself i terrifying predicament, the man who should despise her is the who offers his help.

A romantic adventure for two people looking to heal their broken hearts.

Working together to find the person plotting to ruin their liv Benedict and Cassandra attempt to unravel the pieces of mystery. But when their suspicions circle around friends a family members, the only people they can trust are each other. C they overcome their bitterness and learn to love again? Can th find the villain responsible for their predicament before he dri them apart for good?

ISBN 9781916277403
90000
9 781916 277403